ENLIGHTENED ASCENT

The Pearson Prophecy, Book Two

JEN L. GREY

ENLIGHTENED ASCENT
THE PEARSON PROPHECY, BOOK 2
JEN L. GREY

Power and love come with hard choices.

Afraid the king will find out she's not truly dead, Ariah flees from the kingdom, leaving her family and enemies behind to think the worst. She thinks she's finally struck a bit of luck with the help of a prince, but when he betrays her, she realizes she'd only had a false sense of security.

On the run again, betrayed and in pain, Ariah vows to never be weak again. Soon, she finds herself in another kingdom as an untrustworthy outsider, but she's determined to make it her new home.

However, her fate begins to unravel in the presence of another persistent royal. Now, to fulfill her destiny, Ariah must make a decision as the war looms closer.

Proofread by Jamie Holmes

Edited by Kendra Gaither

Cover Design Eden Elements

Dedication

To my wonderful husband – Thanks for everything!

Chapter One

ᘓᘓᘓ

Tears streak down my cheeks. My best friend is marrying my sister. I love Nick deeply, and Emerson? Well, she's the only sister I have ever known. I look out the carriage window hoping Sam doesn't notice.

Why would the King throw me off the balcony? He hates me, but my sister is the Savior. And Nick was there and didn't help me at all. King Percy would have a fit if he knew that the Prince of Orlon was helping me escape. Sam's taking a big risk helping me, since King Percy is determined to be the ruler of our entire country. He's determined to be the King of Knova, no matter the cost. Thank goodness Sam is still willing to help me.

The palace fades behind us through the rain. I'm leaving a large part of my heart behind. My mother and brother won't know what has happened to me. Will they be told I fell? That I jumped? That I was pushed? Will Claire be able to console my brother enough so that he doesn't get himself into trouble? Will my sister learn the truth, and will she even care? Will I ever see any of them again?

The palace has always looked like a dark place just pretending to be in the light. However, today, it appears truly evil with the darkness and angry clouds shrouding it. The usually radiant white walls are gray, and all the windows shut, keeping the storm out.

I clutch my hands in my lap, welcoming the pain my fingernails bring when pressing against my skin. I glance around the carriage for the first time and take in how extremely gaudy it looks with all its gold trim and emerald jewels. The inside walls are covered in bright yellow silk, like fourteen-carat gold, with dark green stones decorated all throughout. I obviously don't belong here. Where am I going to go, and what am I going to do?

Hearing those wedding bells ring throughout the kingdom as Sam and I pull out the palace gates somehow manages to break my heart further. Even my power isn't coursing through me as normal. I'm not sure if it's due to the hindering powder Elizabeth threw on me, my power beaten down, or a combination of the two. How is that possible after everything that has happened today?

Sam tenses beside me; his brown eyes are full of concern, and he rubs my shoulders. Tremors are coursing through my body, and I lean against the side of the carriage.

He narrows his dark eyes, and clenches his jaw. "Ari, I am so sorry. I don't know what happened this morning, but I am taking you somewhere safe."

I want to laugh, because how can he make that promise? So many people have already hurt me so much that I can't imagine ever recovering. My heart is torn into small pieces and will never be whole.

Nick betrayed me. Of course, my first relationship had to

end in a disaster. Why did I ever let myself believe that our relationship was possible? I'm such a fool.

A nudging sensation from within alerts me of my brother using our bond to connect with me. His hysteria flits through my body, adding to my own. I cut off our link for his safety. If the King even suspects that he knows something or that I'm not dead, there would be hell to pay. Pain slams into my heart like a hundred daggers. A silent scream rips from my throat. My vision blackens and I find relief.

I'm jostled awake and sit up in alarm. I'm not sure how long I've been out, but it seems as if the carriage has stopped. I am being shaken and hear echoes of what sounds like my name. It almost seems muffled. Am I in a cave? I try opening my eyes, but the darkness is about to take me again. A sharp, jolting pain radiates across my cheek. My eyes pop open, and I'm slammed back into reality. The guard is standing beside me in the carriage, and Sam is behind him. What the hell? Why would he not let me stay in peace? Maybe I should return the favor. I look around trying to gather my bearings. The sky now is turning twilight and the rain is moving out, letting some of the stars' light break through. The moon is halfway visible, hidden by the rolling, dark clouds.

Sam's brown hair is in disarray, even though his crown is firmly in place, and his tall body is tense. He pulls the tall, auburn-haired guard out of the carriage and gets in his face. "If you ever touch her again," his tone deepens, "I will kill you myself."

I rise and stumble out of the carriage. I smell the musky scent that the showers left behind, and can hear the animals scurrying, bunkering down for the night. We need to bunker down for the night. I place my hand on Sam's shoulder, trying to calm him. "Whatever he did, it worked."

At my touch, Sam turns around and pulls me into a hug. I sink into his arms, welcoming his comfort. His musky scent calms me. He leans back and touches my cheek. "Are you okay?"

Thank goodness he's here. Right now, I need someone to rely on, and he is being that for me. The sun is now completely out of sight. How is that possible? Just a few minutes ago, it was morning. "How is it almost dusk already?"

Sam runs his hands down his face then places his hands around my waist. This seems wrong, so I take a step back. His face falls, but he stares into my eyes. "Ari, you've been incoherent almost all day. At first, I thought you just needed some time, but when we stopped to bunker down for the night, I couldn't get you to wake. For the first time ever, I was scared."

I open my mouth to apologize, but thoughts from earlier flit through my brain. By now, Nick and Emerson are married. My family either thinks I'm dead or a runaway. Either way, I can't go back, or my entire family will be at risk. How am I going to survive? What am I going to do? I've lost everything. Well, everything but Sam. But, really, how long can he remain with me? He has his own family and kingdom to return to. Then I'll truly be alone. Tears flood my eyes, and once again, I just feel broken.

The guard rushes to me and places his hands on my shoulder. His golden eyes flicker to Sam. "Lay her down before she falls. She's starting to lose it again. I'll set the tent up."

Sam nods and replaces the guard. No, I can't be helpless. I need to help get the area prepped. I focus on taking deep breaths.

Sam sits us on the ground and pulls me into his lap. He plays with my hair and sings softly to me. I've never heard him sing before, and it's actually quite beautiful. His voice is a deep tenor that calms my restless mind.

I've just lost my entire family and best friend. I've been torn away from the only home I've ever known. However, now is not the time to fall apart. I have to figure out what to do. I climb out of his lap. He exhales and touches my hand with a sad smile on his face. "I'm going to make us something to eat. Do you need anything else?"

I take a deep breath and realize I am starving and thirsty. "May I have some water, too?"

His brown eyes sparkle, and he smiles, causing my heart to skip a beat. "Of course, pretty girl. I'll be right back."

I enjoy the moment to myself, where I can think things through without interruption. We are deep in the forest and have found a more level spot to camp for the night. Thankfully, Sam is wonderful. Obviously, I wouldn't be here and alive if he wasn't, but that's the thing. My whole life has been turned upside down. I won't be able to see Logan every day and be there to be part of his wedding. It was always a given that I would be right there in the family section, supporting my brother on that special day. However, I can't put his life at risk over my selfishness even though he is marrying my best friend. He and Claire deserve to have a happy and relatively safe life. My brother has always been my one constant in life, and knowing he is not going to be any longer cuts deep.

Sam sits beside me, pulling me from my thoughts. He hands me a sandwich, while sitting awkwardly on the ground. His royal clothes are bunched up and stiff. He pulls on his pants and then grabs his own sandwich, taking a bite.

Yes, I probably should eat, but before I can eat mine, I

glance at the guard. He hasn't stopped working since we arrived. Or at least that's how it seems. "Aren't you hungry?"

He continues to work, ignoring me.

Since I don't know his name, I'm not sure how to get his attention. I should probably learn it soon. I get up and touch his shoulder.

He startles and looks up at me, his golden eyes narrowed. "Are you okay?"

What's his problem? I haven't done anything to him. Maybe he's hard of hearing? "I asked if you were hungry."

"'Oh." He straightens, glancing at Sam. "Yes. But I will eat later after I get everything settled in for the night."

I wish he would take care of himself. It's custom for the Prince to eat first, but he's traveled just as far as us today. Well, if that's the case, who says I can't help him? I walk around our perimeter and gather wood.

Sam gets up and walks over to me, his forehead creased and his clothes slightly wrinkled. "Ari, what are you doing? Sit down and eat."

Isn't it obvious what I'm doing? I have bark in my hands for goodness sake. "I'm helping Mister... uh, guard, here." I turn and look at the guard. "I'm sorry, I don't know your name."

The guard stops stacking fallen logs and shifts from one foot to another. He clears his throat. "My name is Pierce. But, please, sit down, as Prince Samuel said. I can get everything prepped so you two can get some rest."

"No, absolutely not. I will help you, and then we can eat together. There is no reason why you should be the only one doing all this stuff." I remove my hand from Sam's and grab some more sticks.

Sam has an amused expression on his face as he watches

our exchange. He shakes his head. "All right, Pierce. Ari is right as usual. Let's get this place set up while there is still some daylight. Then, we can all eat together."

Pierce pauses again when Sam comes over to help, but he doesn't object. We all focus on setting camp.

I continue my task of gathering wood for our fire, because that seems like a simple enough task for me.

Pierce and Sam work on erecting the tent. It takes two since the winds are still picked up from the storms. After a short struggle, it's finally standing.

Dumping the sticks in the center of the campsite, I work on getting the fire ready to be lit. I dust off my hands. It feels so good to be working on something.

Sam walks over to me, his face covered in dirt and his crown lopsided on his head.

I laugh. This is the first time I've ever seen him not looking princely. "Come here."

He cuts his eyes over at me, but does as I ask. "What? Is there something on my clothes?"

Of course, that would be what he is concerned with. I attempt to put his crown back in place, but his hair is so messy it won't stay. Why would he wear this out in the wilderness? "You probably should have taken this off."

"You're right. I'm just use to always wearing it."

I turn away from him, reality hitting me hard. This is how different our lives are. I need to learn how to take care of myself. How to make it on my own.

Pierce hasn't stopped working but seems to be paying attention to my and Sam's exchange. After the whole crown debacle, we have the campsite set up rather quickly and twilight has descended. Pierce bends down to light the fire, and I have to bite my tongue. I could light the fire for us quickly, but for some reason, I am hesitant to show them what I can do. Also, I am still drained and am unsure if I can control it well in my state. The powder Elizabeth threw on me still seems to be affecting me.

I grab some food from our bags and make Pierce a sandwich while he works on the fire. By the time his food is ready, the fire is lit. I hand him the food and sit on the ground.

He looks around, and finally makes himself comfortable as well. He gives me a small smile and softly whispers, "Thanks."

Today has been an eventful day. I gaze around our campsite and listen for anything out of the ordinary. This is really my first time camping outside. The wind has thankfully died down and the rain brought a chill to the air. I bet Mother and Logan are sitting down for dinner right now.

How I wish I could be there with them. Why did I risk it all for a stupid boy? Why was I so naïve? I set my sandwich down, needing to get up and move around. I need to do something to distract me or just be by myself, so I can wallow in secret. I excuse myself and head for the carriage.

Sam jumps up with me. He takes my hand, leading me over to the tent. "So… we have a slight problem with the sleeping arrangements."

So, he's finally brought it up. I've been wondering how long it was going take him.

He glances at the carriage. "Well, in our haste to leave, Pierce was only able to grab one tent."

"Yes, I figured that out."

He takes a step toward me and reaches for my hand. "Well, you and I will sleep there, and Pierce will sleep in the carriage."

I really don't care. At this point, I feel safe with Sam. I shrug and shake my head, letting him know it's okay without using words. I shouldn't be okay with this, but after the day I've had, I actually welcome the thought.

We enter the tent, and he heads to the corner and rifles through some luggage. He pulls out a comfy pair of pants and a shirt that appears to be my size. He hands them to me and turns to leave. "I'll be back in just a few minutes."

I change and stare at our cot on the ground. This won't be awkward, right?

After a few moments of hesitation, I crawl in and pull the covers over me, trying to get comfortable.

Soon, Sam walks back in, dressed more casually than I have ever seen him. He is drop-dead gorgeous, dressed in just a plain white shirt and comfortable pants. He seems more like a boy my age than a prince being groomed to lead a kingdom. I scan him from his head down to his toes.

He blushes.

I look away. What is wrong with me?

He snickers as he crawls in beside me and draws me into his arms.

I've always been able to find comfort in them, and I exhale in contentment. I turn to face him.

He touches the part of my cheek that is bruised from where the king had slapped me earlier on the balcony before I was tossed over.

What's strange is that it seems like a lifetime ago at this point, and I'm just so run down.

He gazes in my eyes and says in a husky tone. "If I had been there, Ari, he wouldn't have had the chance to touch you like that."

For some reason, I believe him and scoot closer.

He looks at me in a way that steals my breath. He bends down until his lips are on mine and he is kissing me with such passion that it almost seems desperate.

I meet his intensity, wanting more. We get lost in each other until I'm feeling dizzy. I moan in response, which causes him to growl and roll on top of me. Before anything else can escalate, we hear Pierce clear his throat at the tent's entrance.

Sam groans in agitation, but my mind returns to me.

My feelings for Sam are strong, but that's not the only reason for getting lost in the kiss. I'm looking for a distraction as well as comfort. I can't use him to get over Nick. I need to be fair and wait until I am able to care for him in the same way he cares for me. Pierce hits the tent door, his voice gruff. "Sorry to interrupt, but I need some covers if you don't mind. It's getting cold out here."

Oh my goodness, does he know what was happening in here? I'm so mortified. My voice is shaky. "Sure, come on in. We were just getting ready to fall asleep."

Sam chuckles in my ear. "Is that what this is called? I need to get ready for bed with you more often."

Did he really just say that? How could he make jokes at a time like this?

Pierce walks in and grabs a blanket. He avoids eye contact with us and is in and out of the tent as quickly as possible. That confirms it. He knew exactly what was going on between Sam and me.

Sam laughs and snuggles me closer. "Good night, Ari. See you in the morning."

With that, I fall fast asleep in the comfort of his arms.

Chapter Two

W hen I open my eyes, I am confused. I don't recognize where I am, but then, the day before floods my mind. I quickly realize that I am still wrapped in Sam's arms and that yesterday's events were not some crazy nightmare. The only light at the end of the tunnel is Sam. Our kiss comes to the forefront of my mind. Why did I let things go so far last night? I do have feelings for him. But last night, it was all about just wanting to forget. I cringe at my realization.

Sam snuggles closer and whispers. "Stop thinking and let's just enjoy our time together a few minutes longer. We have another two days of travel before arriving in my kingdom."

His words should be comforting, but they rile me up more. We are leaving the only kingdom I've ever known, and I haven't even thought about where we are going. He is taking me to Orlon. Where will I live? How am I going to make a living? Will I even be able to find a job? They are known for their jewels and silks. All my experience is around farms and animals.

Sam kisses the top of my head. "Obviously, my words offer no comfort." He taps me gently on top of my forehead. "I think I can actually feel your wheels spinning up here."

Now, I feel even worse. I hate disappointing him. He laughs. "Come on, pretty girl. Let's go make some breakfast. Don't worry. I'll make sure Pierce gets some food this time, too."

We crawl out of the tent and walk over to the fire pit.

Sam claps his hands and holds up one finger. "I'm going to get some wood. Be right back."

A few minutes later, he comes back with his hands full of wood, carrying it haphazardly.

I burst out laughing. He is really trying to do normal things, but you can tell he has never done anything like this before.

He sticks his tongue out at me as he lays the wood down. He looks around on the ground.

I walk toward him, puzzled. "What are you doing?"

He scratches his chin. "Well, uh… How do I start a fire?" He picks up two sticks and starts rubbing them together. Nothing is happening, and there isn't a chance that this will work.

I am starving, and against my better judgment, I decide to use my power. I close my eyes and imagine a burst of fire engulfing the wood.

Sam startles, his eyes wide. "What the heck? Did you do that, Ariah?"

Oh, no. I should've went with my gut. "Uh… yes, I did. Sorry, I didn't mean to catch you off guard."

Sam has an unreadable expression. "No, it's fine. It's just, I have never seen anyone be able to light something like that with their powers so controlled. The last time someone tried that in our kingdom, we had a forest fire for days."

How do I respond and downplay what he saw? "Oh, well, I've been training really hard and with one-on-one instruction."

He stares at the fire and lets the conversation drop.

Pierce walks out and gawks at the prince in surprise. "You lit that, Prince Samuel? Good job." His light brown hair is ruffled from sleep, and he seems to be limping, dark circles under his brown eyes. I'm sure the carriage isn't comfortable. He's not as tall as Sam, but definitely thicker from manual labor. He continues to our food supplies and pulls out some eggs and bread. Within minutes, we have breakfast laid out and are eating.

All through breakfast, Pierce watches me.

I am uncomfortable, but I try to ignore the scrutiny.

Sam is about to get up when Pierce speaks up, surprising both of us. "Prince Samuel, you know I will obey and do whatever is needed. I just need to understand what we are running from."

Sam stares at the ground. "Honestly, Pierce, I'm not sure, and I haven't wanted to ask Ariah to talk about this yet. But, you're right. We need to know what's going on."

I take a deep breath, not wanting to have this conversation, but I also realize that it is selfish not to. These two men saved my life, whether they realize it or not. Figuring, at this point, I have nothing to lose, I decide to just be blunt. "King Percy threw me off his balcony after Elizabeth covered me with a powder that would eliminate my power. Due to the intensity of the storm, I was able to tap into the elements and save myself from hitting the rocks or getting washed out with the current. That's when Lydia stumbled upon me. I'm assuming everyone thinks I'm dead except for you two, Lydia, and Hazel." For some reason, it seems imperative that I leave out the part of Lydia saving me from falling to my death. I don't know why, but Hazel said to trust my gut, so I am going with that.

Pierce seems shocked at my story, but Sam just shakes his head in disgust.

Pierce stands and turns toward the tent. "Well, if that's the case, we better get going. King Percy may send his men out since you left right before the wedding, Prince Samuel. It's imperative that we take a different route, one that would be unexpected, or we might have more problems than we need."

Sam rolls his eyes. "Why in Knova would he come looking for me?"

"Because, like it or not, dear Prince, you insulted them by skipping their wedding. He's going to want answers."

Oh, the last thing I want to do is run into him or the guards. I quickly stand to help break down the tent.

Sam must notice that I'm wanting to leave and gets up to help disassemble the tent.

Within minutes, we've packed up our supplies and are heading out. The carriage lurches forward, and after a short while, the ride gets bumpy.

Sam grumbles but doesn't say anything more.

The ride is exactly what I need. The bumps have gotten so hard that I'm focusing entirely on not hitting my head on the sides of the carriage. It keeps me distracted from over-thinking the past few days. Eventually, I am so sore, that I'm ecstatic when the carriage finally rolls to a stop.

Sam opens the door and gets out of the carriage ahead of me to help me down.

The forest around us is more wild and untamed. Wherever we are must be way off the beaten path.

Sam turns in a circle, taking in our surroundings. "Where in the hell are we, Pierce?"

Pierce appears, making his way to us. "Please, calm down, Your Highness. I know exactly where we are. It's just an unused route that will get us to your Kingdom. It will not take any additional travel time, and no one from Agrolon will find us."

I was hoping for a few extra days of travel time. I have to figure out what I'm going to do. I wish Claire and Logan were here with me. Will I ever stop feeling that way? I breathe deeply, trying to calm myself. I need to distract myself. Thinking of them still hurts too much. I make my way toward the back of the carriage where everything is packed.

Sam grabs my hand. "Ari, what are you doing?"

I motion to the three of us. "Well, we are all just looking at each other, so I thought at least one of us could get things moving. The sun is going to set soon, and we have a campsite to build."

Pierce's eyes widen.

Maybe I shouldn't be talking to Sam this way in front of his guard, but I have more serious problems than my tone.

Sam heads over to help me.

Pierce ties up the horses then makes his way to help as well. They unload the tent and food while I attempt to find us a decent portion of level ground. Well, as level as possible.

I find myself away from the others.

Sam notices how far away I am. "Ari, don't go too far. We may be safe from King Percy, but who knows what else is out here."

Even if we do run into something, what is Sam going to do? Command it to leave? I walk through some thick trees, and all of a sudden, I feel a strange nudging inside me, and something has taken a hold of me. It feels similar to my power, but it's different somehow. It pulls me toward the bottom of the hill I was standing on.

I try not to follow, try to turn back as Sam asked, but I can't break loose from the hold. Fear coils around me, but my feet keep moving despite my terror. Sam is calling my name, but I'm at the mercy of the pull. I continue to walk, and after a few more feet, the key on my necklace pulses. It has a white glow pouring out of it at various intervals. Almost as if it's beating to a song I can't hear. It's the weirdest thing but it seems to sync with the energy that has taken over my body.

My feet continue to propel me, and soon, I find myself stumbling upon a large lake in the middle of the forest. As I walk closer to the water, there are houses that blend in with the trees a short distance away. There are large trees surrounding the small houses, but the homes themselves are made of wood similar to how the Pearson house looks.

The force is still pulling me, and I walk around the water until I come to a cave that is hidden by the trees bordering the lake. There is an opening, but right when I'm about to walk inside, a voice calls out, "I wouldn't go in there if I were you."

I turn around, startled. Whatever had a hold on me has vanished, however, the key is still burning.

A lady appears in front of me that could pass as Lydia's twin, but instead of the dark, red hair, she has brown. However, they are about the same height and their eyes are a similar shade of blue.

Oh, I'm staring. I focus my attention on the water. How do I respond to that? "Well, I didn't really want to."

She raises an eyebrow and crosses her arms. "Then, why were you about to walk in?"

I would really love to have an answer to this. It's an excellent question. "I'm not sure."

The key keeps getting hotter, and I hurry to take it off from my neck and drop it on the ground.

The lady's gasps and her eyes grow large. She bends down and picks it up, studying it in her hands. The key thrums, and she winces. She holds it out for me to take and whimpers. "This is yours."

I brace myself for the burn, but it's back to its normal temperature now. I put it back on my necklace and stuff the key inside my top.

She watches me and opens her mouth.

A deep voice interrupts her. "Who the hell do we have here, Willow?" He comes into view, all tall, strong, and arrogant. He has dark brown hair, jade eyes, and he's dressed entirely in black.

His eyebrows rise when he sees me.

My energy pulses inside me, almost as if it wants to connect with him. The longer I stand here, the worse it gets. What is going on? I want to walk toward him.

He glares at me. "Who are you, and what do you want?"

My power is still increasing, spiraling out of control. I'm struggling to control it, so I'm not able to answer.

The guy whistles, and people begin rushing toward the lake, answering his call. It's like they just appeared out of thin air.

He glares at me. "How did you find us? How did you break our barrier?"

Is he crazy? I didn't see anything. "What barrier? Something pulled me here. I didn't mean to upset anyone."

He moves in my direction.

Willow steps in front of him. "She isn't doing anything wrong. The barrier didn't fall, because it recognized her as one of us."

He looks like he's about to argue but stops himself. "Fine, but she needs to go." He turns his jade eyes on me. "We live in secret, and you shouldn't have been able to find us. So, I need you to promise you will keep our location secret. Can you do that?"

I nod. I won't be telling anyone about this.

He brings out a knife. He cuts his hand, making it bleed, then hands the knife to me. When I don't grab it, he grumbles, "Are you going to take it or not?"

I'm not sure what he expects me to do. I don't want to touch that bloody knife.

Footsteps echo and a girl appears next to him. She has matching brown hair and jade eyes. Is that his sister? "Owen, really? She obviously doesn't have a clue what to do. Instead of growling, why don't you explain it to her?" She glares at him. She then turns to me. "He wants you to cut your hand, so you can make a blood promise. Those can't be broken."

What the hell? People actually still do that?

Everyone is watching me.

I want to hide in the shadows, so I reach for the knife, cutting my hand. I whimper at the throbbing pain, and Owen takes a step toward me. His eyes are full of concern. I reflectively move toward him, needing to be closer. My movement makes him pause, and he looks at me in pure disgust.

He reaches his hand out to me, and I cringe but place mine to his.

When we touch, a strong current of power runs through me.

Owen shivers and sucks in a large breath. His tone is loud when he finally speaks. "Say you won't tell them where to find us."

"I promise not to let anyone know."

Owen drops his hands and quickly turns, walking away.

Why does it feel as if he just walked away with half my heart? I've known him for only a brief amount of time.

The girl steps in front of me. She looks me over and tilts her head. "Sorry, my brother's an ass. He's normally not that bad. You must rub him the wrong way. Do you need help finding your way back to your crew?"

I'd love the help, but with how Owen made it clear he wanted me to leave them all alone, I think it will just wind up making things worse. "No, I've got it. Thanks for offering. You're the nicest one here."

She bursts out laughing. "I don't think anyone has ever said that to me. Word to the wise, don't mistake kindness for convenience."

What does that mean? She was offering to help. Wasn't she?

The girl continues to snicker while she turns toward the village. There is a large, blonde man standing close by leaning against a tree. He stares at me until the girl is all the to the village and turns to leave me alone by the water.

Sam's shouting breaks me out of my daze. I walk past the lake and back into the woods, hurrying back to the campsite. When I break through the woods, Sam immediately spots me and moves in my direction.

When he reaches me, he checks me over. "Where the hell have you been, Ari?"

I didn't mean to make him worry. However, I can't tell him the truth, so I reach out to comfort him. "I'm sorry. I thought I saw something and got lost."

He sighs leaning down to rest his forehead against mine. "Do you know how worried I was? You just disappeared, and I couldn't find you anywhere. I think you aged me five years."

I giggle and notice there are small twigs in his hair, his shirt is torn on the sleeves, and there is dirt all over his pants. Despite his tattered appearance, he really is more handsome this way instead of groomed to perfection.

He leans down and brushes his lips against mine. "Come on, let me show you where we decided to set up."

He takes my hand.

I follow behind him. Night is falling fast, and we haven't even started setting up camp. When we arrive back, we work on unloading the carriage. By the time the tent and food are unloaded, Pierce comes back.

Pierce hurries over to us. "Oh, I'm sorry. I was still out looking for you, Lady Ariah."

I smile and touch his shoulder. "It's okay. Sorry if I worried you as well."

He nods and begins setting up the tent while Sam gathers wood for the fire. Luckily, we get everything set up right at dusk. Fortunately, the ground is pretty level, but the tent is stuck in between two trees. The carriage is now at the side and there is a fallen tree that we all plan to sit on.

I open up a few cans of food and hand them out. As soon as Sam takes the food from my hand, he sees the cut from earlier.

Sam frowns and grabs my hand, flipping it over. He finds the cut and it is still oozing blood a little. "What happened?"

How do I salvage this? I can't tell him the truth for many

reasons. "Oh, I cut my hand while I was lost. It just happened. It'll be fine. I just need to clean it tonight."

His forehead creases, and he raises an eyebrow. "You've been in the woods with an open wound. Let's get it cleaned. We can't risk infection."

I hate telling a half-lie, but obviously, it's very important that I keep their secret. He reaches into a bag and pulls out some of our spirits. His brown eyes concerned. "Ari, this is going to hurt like hell."

Of course it is. I brace myself and close my eyes.

He pours it over my wound, and it feels as if my hand is on fire. The pain intensifies and tears pool in my eyes. I hadn't realized how deep I had cut my hand, since I was just trying to get the attention off me.

He grimaces. "I'm sorry."

Pierce must have left, because he comes over with a clean bandage.

I fidget. "Thanks."

They both settle back down and eat so we can go to bed. Once again, Pierce sleeps in the carriage, and Sam and I head into the tent.

He crawls in bed and opens his arms out wide, waiting for me to crawl beside him. I'm out again within seconds.

Chapter Three

I wake up before Sam and try to get up without disturbing him. I need coffee desperately. I head over to where our fire had been lit and reignite it with my powers, thinking no one is around.

Pierce comes out of the forest and pauses. "I've never seen anyone have control like that, and it came easy to you."

He is carrying two rabbits, so he must have just returned from hunting. How did I not hear him? I checked to make sure I was alone. I can't believe he saw me. "Well, my sister is the future Savior. What did you expect?"

He sits the poor white rabbits down, keeping his golden eyes on me. "Yeah, your sister. Not you. Why would you have that much power?"

I shrug. "Well, I'm from the same genes. Maybe I just get a lucky boost."

Thankfully, Sam comes out.

Pierce drops it.

Sam walks over to me and kisses me on the lips. "Morning, pretty girl."

I cringe from his attention and want to move away. What is wrong with me? Why does it feel as if I'm cheating on someone? His kisses have never felt wrong before. What in Knova has changed?

Hurt crosses his face, but he turns his attention to the rabbits. "Is that what we're having?"

Pierce is sitting down with is back propped up against a large tree. He is skinning the rabbits. "Yes, my Prince. A little protein is always a good thing."

Before Sam focuses back on me, I turn and start looking through our food supplies looking for the instant coffee. I'm not a huge fan of this kind of coffee, but beggars can't be choosers.

By the time I walk back over with the drinks, Pierce has the rabbits cooking, and Sam is sitting next to the fire.

Deciding that I should be productive while breakfast cooks, I head over and work on dismantling the tent.

Soon, Sam joins me. "Hey, Ari, what's going on? I mean, the other night, I thought we were on the same page. But this morning, we didn't feel in sync."

I bite my lip. This was inevitable, but something has changed. However, I can't hurt his feelings. He means too much to me.

He stands beside me silent and helps me with the tent.

I have to say something. "I don't know. I just need some time. I just lost my whole family and best friend. I don't want to lead you on, and I think I might have inadvertently done that the other night. You need someone who will love you without doubts, and I'm not that person right now. I'm just trying to survive."

Sam glances at the ground avoiding my gaze and doesn't say a word, so we continue to work in silence. When we are done, Sam touches my arm. "I get it, Ari. Thank you for being honest. Just know you're it for me. I'll wait until you're ready."

I try to smile, but I don't know if I'll ever be ready. However, selfishly, I don't say this. I don't want him to give up on me. I need him. He's all I have left.

Pierce's voice reaches us. "Come and get it."

We head back over to eat our delectable meal of rabbit and berries, then load up the carriage and get ready for another day's travel.

I want to go back to the village and see Owen, but I wouldn't be welcomed, especially with Sam and Pierce in tow. What was in that cave? I wish Willow hadn't interrupted me.

Another day of being bounced around is what is in store. After a while, Pierce stops the carriage, and I am so glad. My body is sore, but I'm not going to complain. If I hadn't been able to sneak out of Agrolon, I'd be dead right now, so sore is something I can deal with.

We stop for lunch and to stretch our legs. We are running low on food, which is to be expected now that our trip has been extended. I bet Logan and Mother are having lunch right now. Thinking of my family hurts so much. All the time we had together that I didn't take advantage of. I would give up everything just to be back there with them.

With meeting Owen and my necklace acting strange, I'd managed to stay distracted, but once again, my thoughts catch up. Nick and Emerson are on their honeymoon, with Logan, my mother, and Claire left wondering what happened.

I'm sure Mother and Logan know something happened. After all, they were there when Elizabeth knocked on our door asking for me to walk with her that morning, leading me to what was supposed to be my death. However, Nick telling me he didn't want me, and then the King pushing me off that balcony, is something I'll never forget. Bitterness swirls inside me, and I welcome it. Anything is better than pain.

Pierce watches me with concern in his eyes, and Sam is gazing around taking in the forest.

I glance around and realize that the trees aren't as close together. I wonder if that means we're approaching Noslon? The next phase of my life is just about to begin.

I busy myself, needing a distraction from thinking of my future and how I'm going to live. I grab several small sandwiches and hand them out. We eat in silence, but when Sam finishes, I can tell he's not full. He's eyeing my sandwich, and his stomach grumbles.

Pierce finished his meal and clears his throat. "We will make it into the eastern part of your kingdom tomorrow, Your Highness."

At those words, Sam relaxes. However, the complete opposite happens to me. Where am I going to live? How am I going to make a living? Panic claws at me and I begin taking deep breaths. I'll figure something out, and getting all upset won't change a thing.

We head north again for a while, until sunset, then we quietly get everything set up for the night and head to bed.

When I walk into the tent, Sam smiles at me. "I can't wait until we get to my kingdom tomorrow. I've wanted you to see my land ever since I laid eyes on you that night at the arrival dinner. Actually, I spend most of my time in the eastern portion away from the palace. It's exquisite and just a few hours' travel if I need to make an appearance at the castle. We will actually go to my house."

I force a smile. He has a house, but I don't. I don't even have any coins. Tremors are racking my body and my palms are getting sweaty. Of course, he's happy to be home, but it isn't my home.

He reaches out and takes my hand.

"What's wrong, Ari?"

How do I explain this to him? Doesn't he realize the situation I'm in? "Sam, I am glad you want me to see your kingdom, but I have no home. I'll need to get a job and find a place to stay as soon as we get there."

His mouth opens half way. "Ari, this is what you've been worried about?" He reaches for my hand, his tone sincere. "I am so sorry. If I hadn't been so excited, I would have noticed. You have absolutely nothing to worry about. You'll stay with me, and I'll take care of you."

I shake my head forcefully. "No, I can't do that. I won't take advantage of you. I'll figure something out, I'm sure. I'm just so thankful that you saved me."

He gets up from the cot and walks toward me, wrapping his arms around my waist. "Ari, I want to take care of you. I intend to make you mine in every way. How else can I prove this?"

Being in his arms feels nice. Maybe I'm not using him for comfort. Maybe he is the real deal. Why did I waste all my time and tears on Nick when Sam has been waiting all this time? For once, someone wants to take care of me. Before I realize what's happening, his lips are on mine again. Desperation and longing fill me, and I channel it into our kiss. Each nip and stroke is returned. We stumble to the cot, and he lies down on top of me, running one hand along my side while he uses the other to hold his weight off me. I moan and arch into him, wanting to be closer. My brain becomes foggy, and all I can smell and taste is him. He starts to slide his hands inside my shirt when my power decides to course through me, burning.

He scrambles from the cot, his eyebrows furrowed. "Ari, what the hell? You're burning up. Are you okay?"

As soon as we are not in contact, my body begins to cool. It's as if that was the intent.

Sam closes his eyes and opens them. He places his hand over his eyes. "You're glowing and it's so bright that it's hurting my eyes."

I glance down and see exactly what he is talking about. My skin is bright as if you can see the energy inside me, but the glow is already dimming. I can only imagine what I looked like moments ago.

He opens his eyes and reaches out, touching me carefully. "Thank goodness. You're not hot anymore."

Exhaustion is pulling me down, and I'm thankful that I'm already lying down.

He comes over to me and lays on the edge of the cot.

He has never stayed away from me like that. Has he changed his mind? When Nick had acted like this, it had marked the beginning of the end for us. That was when he told me he'd been set to wed my sister. I've got to figure out what is going on with me in every way. What the hell just happened? Am I using Sam for comfort, or do I really feel something for him?

Concern outlines Sam's face. "Ari, are you okay? What's wrong?"

I cover my face with my hands. "I'm a freak and so confused."

He tugs me against him.

I turn over, facing him, and bury my face in his chest.

He strokes my hair. "Oh, pretty girl. I was afraid you were still hot, and I didn't want to make you feel uncomfortable. I will always be here for you. Nothing will change that."

I relax, allowing my body to rest. For some reason, as I fall asleep, Lydia's words keep echoing in my mind. *"Sam's an ally. At least for now."*

She's been right about everything so far. I hope she's wrong about this.

Chapter Four

The hard travel has made each of us sore and stiff. I swear, it feels as if we've been on the road for weeks, but it's actually only been a few days. We eat a light breakfast, eager to get moving. We work on packing up camp, knowing we should arrive at the Kingdom of Orlon, Sam's home, by lunchtime.

Before we leave, Pierce says he needs a minute, so Sam and I finish at the campsite. Pierce walks into the forest and returns with some bright red berries.

He grabs a bowl and puts the berries in it. With a large, thick stick, he starts mashing them.

Sam scratches his head. "What in Knova are you doing? We still have food if you're hungry."

Pierce narrows his eyes. "Do you really think we can take her into the Kingdom like this?"

Sam waves his hand toward me. "Of course, there is absolutely nothing wrong with her."

Pierce lets out a disgusted grunt. "How many girls have you ever seen with black hair?"

My heart sinks. He's right. How am I supposed to live anywhere when I stand out from everyone? What am I going to do? My hands get sweaty and my breath shallow.

Pierce holds out the bold tilting it toward us. "These berries will tint her hair so it appears to be dark red. The longer the berries stay in her hair, the more they will tint her hair. Granted, it will be a really dark red, but it should hide the black."

Is that possible? For the first time, will I be able to walk down a road and just blend in? Why hasn't anyone ever told me about this before?

He sets down the stick and comes over to me, gesturing at my hair. "May I?"

I nod, and Pierce sets the concoction down. He rifles through our bags until he pulls out a towel to put around my shoulders.

He then rubs the gunk all through my hair, and it smells sweet. He works diligently working in sections to ensure it's all covered. After completing the last little bit, he stops running his fingers through my hair and stands. "Okay, it needs to set for some time. Just stay still, and I'll be right back. I need to go wash my hands."

Sam is pacing and running his hands through his hair.

"What's wrong?"

He looks at me. "Oh, nothing, I just love your black hair and honestly, I'm eager to get home. I know we need to dye your hair for your safety, as well as mine, but I will miss seeing the real you. However, I can't wait to see you in my country."

And I thought I was dramatic? However, I can't wait to be able to look at myself in the mirror. What will my hair look like? Will it be hard to get this gunk out of my hair? I wait for

Pierce to return. The berry mixture is starting to get a little crusty and I want it out of my hair. Pierce comes back.

He cleans up the mess he made and gives me the go-ahead to wash it out of my hair. I head over to a small pond a little way away and start working on getting the mashed berries out. It's actually really hard to do, but that's a good thing, right?

When I walk back over to the guys, Pierce has a huge smile on his face. "It looks red wet. That's a good sign. Let's go."

We travel for a while, and eventually, the forest thins. I can see the village in the distance.

Sam can't keep a smile off his face. After some time, we go through the village. The houses are multiple colors and made of gorgeous stones. They are right next to one another, and nicely dressed people are milling around. As we pass, the young children chase us, and the parents smile and wave.

Soon, the houses become farther and farther apart, and eventually, we pull up to a large, gray stone house. It is gorgeous, and in the back is a fountain that appears to be the center of a beautiful garden.

Sam chuckles.

I turn to him, puzzled.

He climbs out of the carriage and helps me down. Once settled, he gestures toward the garden. "You've already noticed the garden. I've been so excited to show it to you. I hope you love it more than the one you left behind."

My eyes sting with the tears trying to form. I didn't leave the garden behind. It was yanked from me. How I wish I was still there with Logan, Claire, and Mother.

Sam must see the grief in my eyes, because he grabs my arm and pulls me into a huge hug.

I bury my face in his chest, breathing him in. He is my rock, and I'm so grateful for meeting him. He is truly one of the best friends someone could have.

After a few moments, someone clears their throat.

Too my surprise, there are at least fifteen people lined up outside of the entrance, just staring. I hate being the center of attention and my body goes rigid.

Sam looks up and notices. "Don't worry. That's just the staff. They are here to greet us and take care of our things," he whispers.

Once again, his words should be comforting, but I'm extremely uncomfortable. It doesn't help that I was buried in his arms. I step out of his arms, trying to gain my composure.

The man in the middle walks toward us. "My Prince, I expected you to be home earlier. The queen stopped by this morning looking for you and seemed very concerned with your absence."

Immediately the Sam I met at Agrolon returns and the boy my age gone. He stands straight and meets the man's eyes. "Well, we ran into a mishap, but no worries. We are fine. Please, take my Lady's things to our best guest room. She will be staying with us, and no one is to say a word. Is that understood?"

The man takes a step back and bows. He turns to the other staff outside and waves a younger man to our luggage while gesturing the others to return inside. A girl about my age stays outside, standing by the door.

Sam pulls me aside and lowers his voice. "I must go see Mother, or she will be down here shortly. I think it's best if she doesn't know you are here yet. I'll be back in time for dinner. Please, make yourself at home. This is your place now."

When I look up, the girl walks up to me. She is a pretty, young girl with dark blonde hair. She is slightly taller than me and has kind brown eyes.

She curtseys. "Please, follow me, miss."

We walk into the mansion, and the door has the Orlon symbol surrounded by emeralds. As we walk through the house, emerald-encrusted lamps, gold-woven rugs, and dark cherry furniture are key decorations throughout each room. The colors are vibrant and beautiful. I've heard stories of their vibrancy, but seeing it for myself is amazing.

There is a large family room and a den that we walk through before we enter a hallway that leads to a spiral staircase. We pass the staircase and continue down the hall until the girl stops and walks into a room.

I join her in the room and notice a huge cherry wood canopy bed with dark emerald green sheets and fabrics taking up one wall. Sliding doors open up to a beautiful patio that overlooks and steps right down into the magnificent garden. There is a large marble bathroom to the left, bigger than my bedroom in Agrolon, with a walk-in shower and tub that is so big I could stretch my arms and legs out. It's breathtaking.

The girl smiles. "You must not be used to having a room like this."

I can't believe I forgot she was in the room. Crap, she must think I've never been in a palace before. "Honestly, I'm used to a nice room, but this is absolutely stunning."

She curtseys once more. "Yes, it is. My name is Emily. Please, let me know if you need anything. I'm sure you want to get clean and rested. The seamstress will be by shortly to make you some clothes, per the prince's orders."

Why would Sam tell them to make me dresses? I really

don't want to deal with that, and right now, a good cleaning sounds nice. I realize I didn't say anything to her before she left. I hope she doesn't think I'm rude.

I walk into the bathroom and turn the water on in the tub. There are some soaps and shampoos sitting on the side of the tub, so I pick up the bottles and look at them, finding jasmine, my favorite. I pour some into the tub and soak, trying to relax my tired, sore muscles. Being jerked around in the carriage was brutal.

I'm not sure how long I've stayed in here, but I probably need to get out. Dragging myself out of the relaxing water, I walk into my room and find someone there rifling through my things. Who is that? Thankfully, I have a towel around me.

She's an older, tall lady with graying, light red hair. She has gowns everywhere, and a measuring tape is on the bed.

She raises her gaze when she hears my entrance and speaks in a very energetic tone. "Hello, miss, my name is Mary. I am so excited to design your dresses. It's been so long now since the queen doesn't stay here. Luckily, I have a few made for random guests that may show up, and they appear to be your size. This will get you by until I can make some solely for you." She gestures toward the middle of the room. "First, let's measure you, and then we will try the other ones on. Please, stand in front of the mirror."

I don't want to do this. I head toward my bags, wanting to put some clothes on as soon as possible. "Oh, let me put some clothes on first."

She holds out her hand, indicating I should stop. "Actually, it's best if you are undressed for precise measurements. I promise I'll make it quick."

My hands tremor as I follow her request. This is very

uncomfortable for me. She'll notice the scars from the king's punishments. Panic claws its way through me, but I make myself take a few deep breaths. It's going to be okay, because my scars disappeared at my Enlightenment. They're gone. It's so hard for me to remember that.

She doesn't say a word, just takes the measurements as promised. As soon as she's done, she motions toward the gowns on the bed. "Please, try these on."

The last thing I want to do is wear those dresses, but she stands there, watching me with a raised eyebrow, just waiting. I have no choice. Relenting, I walk over to the bed and pick a light blue dress. I want to wear pants, but don't want to bring any additional attention.

She helps me slip it on and ties the straps in the back. When I turn around, she smiles. "I knew he would always choose a dark red-haired, beautiful girl."

Of course, her focus would be on my hair color. I wish for once people would actually take notice of a person's character, but that's not the world we live in. Who cares if I treat Sam well as long as my hair is the perfect shade.

She points her finger at me, clearly unhappy. "You know, most people say thank you when they're complimented."

How is that a compliment? It's more of an observation, isn't it? However, her eyes stay on me and I want to disappear.

She laughs. "The other dresses are the exact same size, so they will work in the meantime. The prince will be back soon. Dinner starts at six, so please, don't be late."

After she walks out the door, I pull my hair into a twist and head out to the gardens. As soon as I step into the sun's rays, I relax, and my energy springs to life. Thankfully, it appears that the powder has worn off. My power is thrumming inside me again.

The garden is breathtaking. The flowers are shades of blue, purple, and orange I have never seen. I walk over to a patch of sky blue bulbs that remind me of Claire's eyes. How I miss my spunky, best friend. I bend down to touch them when someone clears their throat. I turn and find Sam standing there with a wide smile. Unfortunately, he has ditched his traveling clothes and is dressed in stiffly-pressed royal garments. He's still handsome, but in a very different way.

"You being here in my garden is like a dream come true." His brown eyes are bright and he's looking at me in awe. "I never thought it would come to fruition. I've never noticed before, but is blue your favorite color?"

I look down and realized that I'm standing next to blue flowers. Thoughts of Claire just keep running through my head. "Yes, it actually is."

He grins and then holds his arm out. "May I escort you to dinner? It's time, and the servants don't like for their hard work to get cold."

I nod and walk to him, placing my arm in his. We make our way slowly through the garden, and I'm more content than when I arrived.

When we enter the dining room, I'm surprised at how small it is. There is one table, but only a small section on the corner is set. It seems intimate. The table could probably feed up to twenty people. However, the beautiful craftwork and linens make up for the less ornate meal. They are emerald, with accents of a dark, rose red in the corners.

I run my hands over the linens, finding them extremely soft.

"Where do the servants eat?"

Sam pulls my chair out and turns his body toward me. "We don't have to make every meal a grand show. They eat in the kitchen, and we eat here. I rather like the solitude."

I eat my meal and attempt to ignore how it's rubbery and tasteless. I just need to focus on accepting my new life with no complaints.

Sam begins eating and makes a disgusted face. "Please save me from this meal."

I giggle, and I'm surprised by the sound. It's been days since the last time I laughed.

Sam's face relaxes, and until then I hadn't noticed all the worry that had lined his face here lately. He pouts playfully. "In order for this meal to be a little more bearable, how about a quick kiss?"

I asked for time, but how can I say no at his cute request. I lean over and quickly brush my lips against his cheek. His request was for more, but that's all I have to offer at this point.

After a little while, I've finished my meal and placed my napkin on the table.

He frowns and takes my hand in his. "I'm sorry our food isn't as good as what you are accustomed to."

I smile at him. "It was perfect. Thank you."

He shakes his head. "Oh, Ari, don't lie. It's okay. I'll make it up to you by spoiling you in every way possible."

Is he crazy? I squeeze his hand. "You don't need to make up for anything. Thank you for saving me."

He reaches out and touches my cheek. "I'll never hurt you and will protect you. This, I promise with all my heart."

Leaning down, he brushes his lips against mine.

For some unknown reason, Owen pops into my head. I

pull away and bite my lip. "I'm so sorry, Sam. I just need time. It's only been a few days."

He leans his head back against the chair. "No, look. I'm sorry. I'm not trying to pressure you, but having you here is a dream come true. I can make you happy if given a chance. I just need you to realize it."

I glance up and notice that several people have entered the room. How long have they been in here? Did they hear our conversation? I'm being paranoid, but I feel as if their eyes are on me.

Sam takes my hand, lifting me from my seat. We leave the dining room and once again head back outside.

Why would the stranger I had only spoken to for a few minutes pop into my mind during an intimate moment? We make it outside, and the fresh air hits me. We make our way to a spot in the garden that has a bench next to some beautiful orange flowers.

After getting comfortable, I turn to him. "What did your mother want?"

He groans and buries his face in my shoulder. "She was worried and angry with me. Angry that I ran out of the wedding, but worried about the reason behind it. I told her that I had gotten word that someone was in danger and needed to be brought back to our kingdom. I made it sound like one of our travelers, so she has no clue you are here. However, I have to write the king and prince to apologize."

So he knows what happened that day. Despite my fear, I need to know what happened. "So, did anyone ask about me at the wedding?"

Sam lifts his head back up and brushes his fingers down my cheek. "Your mother, brother, and friend were going crazy, but apparently, the king took them to their chambers.

They left still angry, but didn't make a scene. And yes, your sister and Prince Nicholas are now wed. I'm sorry, but I knew the prince was too much of a coward to stop the ceremony."

He's right. I wanted to know, but he's not sorry. He has made it clear that he wants me. What hurts worse is that I was a complete fool, believing everything that Nick said. Why was I so stupid?

Sam bends down so we are at eye level. "I'll never betray you, Ari. I want you to be mine."

I close my eyes. Oh, how I want to feel the same way and want to believe him.

Chapter Five

I slept fitfully in the oversized bed, but it wasn't for lack of comfort. Being in a strange place, with so much going on, and worrying about my family and best friend had me tossing and turning most of the night.

I have just gotten dressed when there is a knock on my door. Much to my delight, Sam is there, rolling a breakfast tray in for us to eat together. He's brimming with excitement.

His face is ecstatic. "I'd like to take you for a horseback ride and to tour the village today."

He's so cute and proud, so, of course, I can't say no. We quickly eat then walk out to his stables. There is a beautiful grey stallion out in the middle of the field.

Sam notices what has captured my attention. "Oh, Ari, no. He's wild. My best trainers are struggling to train him."

I ignore him and move closer to the beautiful creature. The stallion and I lock eyes, and my power thrums through me again. I stay still, not wanting to alarm him, and he slowly turns and walks toward me. Sam is saying something to me, but I can't focus on him.

The horse comes to me and slowly puts his head down to where we are at eye level. I reach out and stroke him, and he blows in my face. We stay like that for a minute, until he becomes startled and backs away. I turn around and realize that Sam is getting closer. The stallion takes off, and I wish he hadn't left.

Sam is looking at me with the strangest expression. "How'd you do that? No one has been able to get close to him."

"I didn't do anything. I just wanted to pet him."

Sam smiles at me while shaking his head while turning to head to the stables. "Ari, the strangest things happen to you. It's kind of amazing but still unsettling all the same. Come on, the stablemen should have our horses prepared."

I follow behind him, but take one more glance to ensure the stallion isn't coming back. I'd really like to ride him.

❧

The trip to the village is pretty and uneventful. The forests here aren't nearly as lush as they are in Agrolon, but that's to be expected. Orlon's lands aren't fertile for food and produce, but they thrive at mining and sewing instead.

The village has a nice feeling, though, and the houses are prettier than the ones back home. The stones are colorful, and each house has its own signature style. Sam pulls me toward a large, golden, stone building. When we walk in, I'm not sure what to look at first. There are cases and cases of jewels of all different colors and gold everywhere. I'm so overwhelmed by all the gorgeous designs, I try to take in everything.

I've seen jewelry before, but this is more than that. It is elaborate, beautiful art. They have rings, watches, earrings — anything you can imagine. Sam leads me toward a back room where guards are hovering at the door. They let us in without a problem. He is the prince after all.

He walks over to the case and looks at some intricate bracelets. There is one that is pure gold with their signature green jewels strategically placed all around it. He waves a person over. "Will you please let her try this on?"

The lady smiles and unlocks the case to pull it out.

I'm not sure what he's doing, but he takes it from the lady's hand and places it on my wrist. His smirk is breathtaking. "It looks perfect. We will take it."

The lady nods and pulls out the paperwork.

I can't believe he just bought me this gorgeous bracelet, and I'm not sure what to do. I don't want to say no and reject his gift, especially in front of people. However, it's just too much.

We walk out the door, and I glance at him. "Sam, I love this, I do, but this is too much."

He grins and turns it into an unsuccessful pout. "Not for you. I've wanted to get you something, and what better way than to have my kingdom's color around your wrist. It's rude to reject a gift, Ari. You don't want to hurt my feelings, do you?"

Of course, he's right, and I do love it. It just seems like he's trying to force something on me, and I'm not sure what it is.

Trying not to focus on this, I look around the village and notice everyone milling around. Even the villagers are dressed in fine clothes. Some even have nicer dresses than I had. The women all wear long dresses, and the men wear tailored suits. We walk around the town, and everyone seems to really like Sam. His people actually seek him out and speak to him. I'm introduced to so many people that I become dizzy.

Sam knows when I've had enough. He holds my hand as we make our way back toward the mansion, this time without stopping to talk to people. He just waves as we pass instead. My heart warms at the whole experience.

On our ride back to the mansion, Sam turns to me. "So, did you enjoy your trip?"

"Yes, I really did. Your people really love you, which is so nice to see. No one ever acts like that with our king."

Anger flashes across his face and his tone is rigid. "He's not your king anymore, Ari. Just remember that."

His comment hurts. Why would he say such a thing? I get that I can't go back, but it's been less than a week. It still doesn't seem real. Have I done something to upset him?

I stay quiet the rest of the trip, not sure what to say or how to feel. Sam is usually attuned to my feelings, so I'm a little unsettled by the abrupt change. Walking back into the mansion, I'm tense and a little overwhelmed. I walk to my room, and he heads in the opposite direction, not saying a word. I pour myself a bath and try to wash the day away.

After getting dressed, I contemplate just skipping dinner. I'm hungry, but I don't want to face him. I've learned it's best to hide from tension, because facing it head on only results in retaliation. I lay down on the bed with another uncomfortable dress on. All my pants and shirts have disappeared. I'm not a huge fan of Sam's seamstress. I'm just dozing off when there is a knock at my door.

I get up and open the door.

Sam is leaning on the wall behind him, his head drooping, which is very unlike him.

Normally he's confident and composed, so to see him like this throws me off kilter. What do I say? There is awkward silence which makes me feel the need to say something. "Oh, hi."

He moves toward me with a tight smile, and his eyes are filled with pain. "Are you not joining me for dinner?"

"Oh, I'm not really hungry. I am exhausted from our day out."

He leans against the door frame. "Look, I deserve this. You're lying about being hungry, and I'm sorry. I was a jerk earlier. It's just, I have you here with me at my home, protecting you in a way that coward never did, and you're still talking about the person who tried to kill you as your king. I got jealous. I want you to see that I'm better for you than him."

He seems remorseful and has a pleading look on his face.

I'm so relieved that my Sam is back. "It's okay. I'm just not used to you treating me like that. I don't mean to hurt your feelings, but he's been my king for all my life, and that only changed this past week. Nick was my childhood friend. Besides my brother, he was my only friend for many years. It took a long time before anything ever happened between us. I just need time, but I'm grateful for everything you've done."

He comes over and gives me a hug. He steps back and pulls me out of the room. "Let's go eat. I'm starving."

The meal is once again barely edible. The wait staff really tries hard, but there is only so much you can do when all of your food relies on the mood of the Agrolon King. None of it is fresh, so the flavor is almost gone by the time it arrives in the kingdom. Their texture is off, too, which makes it barely palatable.

As we are leaving the dining room, Sam pulls me close. "Would you please accompany me in the garden?"

I love the garden, but right now I need time alone in my room. I don't want to upset him again so I'm hoping he understands. "I would love to, but, Sam, I'm really tired. Today was fun and overwhelming. I was hoping to go to bed early and get some extra sleep. Can I spend time in the garden tomorrow?"

Disappointment flashes in his eyes, but he smiles sweetly, putting me more at ease. "Of course. It has been a day. Can we spend tomorrow together?"

I want to ask *What else do I have to do?* but know it's not his fault I'm in this situation. So, I smile. "Sounds great."

When we arrive at my door, I turn to him, and he caresses my cheek with his hand. "You don't know how happy I am to have you here. I never dreamed this would happen. It's brought you a lot of pain, but this is a miracle for me. I'll be here bright and early. Sleep well, pretty girl."

I shut the door and change into my pajamas. I pull the curtains open, so I can see the gardens from my bed. The moon is high, and the sky is clear. I really wish I felt up to going outside with Sam, but exhaustion has slowly been taking over all day. I crawl into bed and quickly fall sound asleep.

I wake up, and something seems off. I'm weightless and floating. I look around and realize that I don't have a body. What the hell is going on? I'm surrounded by trees, and it's extremely dark. I'm moving fast, and suddenly, the lake and cave from the village comes into view that I had stumbled upon during our journey to Orlon. Next to the cave is Willow, just like she stood the other day. She has something in her hands, and she's leaning over it, murmuring something I can't make out.

The gorgeous guy steps out of the shadows and into the moonlight. "Mother, what are you doing?"

What? Is Willow his mother?

She looks up and shakes her head. "You messed up by letting her go."

He leans his back against the cave and leans his head back. "We've gone over this a million times. She's not one of us. I'm not sure how she got through the barrier, but I've strengthened it. It won't happen again."

Willow straightens up and marches over to him. "You've made a mistake. She was meant to be here. She was alone and trying to go into the cave, boy. You should listen to me."

He reaches out, trying to take her hand. "Mother, you know you've been sick. The Savior is locked away with the Agrolon king. No one is coming to save us. You have to let this go."

She points her finger at him and scowls. "I'm not crazy. I know you all think that. There is change coming, Owen, and you need to be prepared for it. I may be old, but I'm still aware and know things that I can't explain to you. You shouldn't have let her go, and you shouldn't have forced the blood promise. That was a mistake. You've screwed up. I just hope we can fix this."

I hadn't noticed how close I was until Willow stopped moving and looked around.

"Mother, what are you..." Owen starts.

"Shh..." she cuts him off.

She smiles and somehow finds me. Looking directly into my eyes, she tells me, "My son was rude to you, but know you are welcome here. He may act like he's in charge, but I have the final word."

Then, I'm startled awake.

Chapter Six

My heart is racing, and my breathing is erratic. What the hell just happened? I look down and find that I'm back in my body and on the bed. That had to be a crazy nightmare. However, the chill I get thinking about Willow looking me in the eyes as she talked to my floating presence confirms it was real. Why would I be dreaming about Owen and Willow? Was I even dreaming?

It's still black outside so I get up and turn on the lights, trying to calm down. I've never experienced anything like that before, and paranoia is setting in.

I head to the kitchen, hoping to find some milk to warm. I'm more tired than prior to falling asleep. I find Pierce sitting there at the servant's table.

He notices me and quickly stands. "Are you okay, Ariah?"

He's the last person I thought I'd find there, but eventually, my brain catches up, and I start talking. "Yeah, just a bad dream. I thought you stayed with the queen. Is everything okay?"

He bites his lip. "Yes, everything is fine. The queen

wanted me to come here and let Prince Samuel know that he needs to visit in the next day or two. I'm here to ensure that it happens."

"Oh, why wouldn't he go?"

Pierce sits on the table's edge and runs his hands down his face. "Ariah, in general, the prince tries not to visit them unless absolutely needed. I volunteered to stay and bring him back, because I'm concerned that he will refuse to go this time unless I'm here to enforce it."

Oh, no. Does anyone realize I'm alive? "Does the queen know I'm here?"

His eyes widen and he stands. "No, I promised I wouldn't tell anyone, and I haven't. I came because Sam is paying you a lot of attention and doesn't want to leave your side. We don't want the queen to come here and find you. I'm here to remind him of that."

I nod my head and just think about all the trouble I've become. I should probably wear a sign that says *'beware'*, but that might garner additional unwanted attention. "Thank you for keeping me safe."

He shakes his head. "You're one of the nicest people I've ever met. I have no clue why so many people hold a grudge against you. You treat others with kindness and expect nothing in return. I am honored to help you in any way possible."

My eyes moisten, so I look for cups and milk, trying to distract myself. After finding everything, I warm some milk for both of us on the stove. I pour the warmed milk into two cups and hand one over to him. He takes it, smiling. "See, you are kind."

I laugh, and we drink our milk in silence. When I'm done,

I set it down. "Thanks so much. Goodnight. I'll see you in a couple of hours."

He nods, and I go back to my room. Hopefully, I can get a couple hours of peaceful sleep.

༺༻

Thankfully, Sam doesn't wake me super early. It's about ten when there is a loud knocking on my door. Luckily, I am completely rested, despite my weird night.

I open the door, and Sam is looking handsome and ready to go. He grins widely. "You're still in your night clothes?"

Did I really just answer the door in my nightgown? I look down, completely mortified. "Yes, sorry. I didn't sleep well. Can you give me a few minutes to change?"

He takes a step back, his eyes light with humor. "Of course, just please hurry. I'm ready for us to start our day."

I find a dress that seems more comfortable than the others and slip it on, making sure that my necklace is secure and hidden under the top. I pull my hair up into a bun and put a little mascara on.

When I walk out of the room, he is leaning against the wall and scans me over. "I swear, you'd look good in rags."

Why does it seem like everyone focuses on my appearance? I'm self-conscious, so this just makes things awkward. I fidget and change the direction of our conversation. "So, what are we doing today?"

His face lights up, and I swear it's the happiest I've ever seen him. "Well, I figured that our kingdom tour tired you out, so maybe we could do a horse ride and have a picnic in the garden."

I smile. "That sounds perfect."

We hurry to the stables and quickly leave on our horses. He shows me where the mines are, where they find the material for the silks, and so many other things. It's fascinating how their kingdom works.

After our tour, we head back to the garden for our lunch. I'm surprised to find the blanket already laid out with food and drinks prepared for us. I glance at him, bewildered.

He laughs and motions toward the picnic. "I told you I had a plan."

I stick my tongue out at him and grab at the food. I'm starving, which makes me realize I skipped breakfast.

Sam watches me for a minute before tearing into the food himself.

When I'm done, I lay back on the blanket, closing my eyes and enjoying the sun on my face. My power is buzzing, and I relish the sensation. I sense Sam laying down beside me and scoot closer to him.

He snickers and turns to hold me. He plays with my hair, and for the first time in a long while, I am content. Being here in his arms eases the pain. Maybe I can love him the way he wants me to.

Running his fingers along my arm, he softly promises, "I am so glad you are here with me. I'll make you happy. You'll see."

Goosebumps rise on my arms, and I snuggle deeper into him.

After some time, I sense the sun going down, so I open my eyes to find that Sam has fallen asleep. I try to wiggle out of his arms without bothering him, but as soon as I'm moving, his eyes pop open.

"Hey, where are you going?"

I bend down and softly pat his cheek. "I'm going to get up and stretch. I've laid still way too long."

He nods, releasing me.

I stretch and am rejuvenated. This was the type of day I needed. The last time Logan and I hung out at the stream pops into my head, but I desperately try to repress the memory. There is no reason to think of painful things since I can't change them. One day, when I'm stronger, I'll be able to remember those happy times.

Sam sits up, his forehead wrinkled. "Hey, what's going on? Your entire demeanor just changed."

I force a smile. "No, I'm good, just trying to work out all the knots. Surprisingly, I'm hungry again. I guess lying around increases my appetite."

He stands and holds his hand out. "Well, then, we better take care of that. I think it's dinner time anyway."

When we walk in the dining room, I find that he is right. The food is being set out, and dinner is ready to eat. We sit down and quickly eat another meal, enjoying each other's company.

After finishing, Sam takes me to a part of the mansion I've not visited before that boasts a library, and I'm surprised at the magnitude of books they have there. The room is huge with bookshelves lining every wall. Every one of them is filled with books, and there are two circular, dark cherry tables in the middle of the room. Sitting at one is Pierce.

Sam stops in his tracks. "Pierce, I didn't realize you were here."

Pierce lays his book down on the table. "Yes, I was going to look for you tonight. Your mother has requested your presence first thing tomorrow morning."

Sam crosses his arms. "Oh, I can't do that. I planned on

taking Ari over to the next village so she can see some of the swords they make there. Tell her I'm sorry and that I'll come soon."

"Sir, I'm not sure you understand. She's not requesting. It's actually a demand."

Sam grunts and tenses. "Fine, I guess I don't have much of a choice then."

Pierce stands. "I just came to deliver the message. She's expecting you by brunch, so let's leave at eight in the morning."

Pulling me out of the room, Sam looks behind him. "Fine, well, I better be getting to bed then."

He walks me to my room and stops at the door. "I'm so sorry, but it seems I'll be occupied tomorrow. Since I need to wake up early, I'm calling it a night. I'll return for dinner tomorrow, and we can spend the evening in the garden if that works for you?"

I grin and nod. "Sounds perfect. Honestly, going to bed early sounds heavenly. I hope you have a good trip tomorrow. Please, be safe."

He kisses me on the lips. "Goodnight."

I close the door and lean back against it. That kiss just didn't feel right. What's going on? I've had feelings for him since I first met him, but ever since my run-in with Owen, things have become more complicated. How is that possible? My head is about to explode, so I quickly change into my pajamas and lay down. Thankfully, I fall asleep fast, and it's a deep, dreamless sleep.

Chapter Seven

I walk into the kitchen the next morning in search of coffee, and the staff instantly pauses and becomes silent. Please, tell me I'm dressed. I glance down and, thankfully, see that I am. After a few more moments of awkward silence, my mouth just begins moving. "Can you please point me in the direction of the coffee?"

An older man bows to me. "Oh, miss. Go to the dining room, and we will gladly serve you. We'll bring you some breakfast. It's ready. We were just waiting for you to come down."

I walk further into the room not wanting to be waited on. "Oh, no. It's fine. I can get it myself."

The man steps in front of me blocking my path, his tone desperate. "Please, miss. This is our job."

I really don't want them to have to wait on me, but at the same time, I don't want to be insulting. I shake my head and give him a small smile. "Okay, that sounds perfect. Thank you."

I walk into the dining hall and sit at the table all by

myself. I haven't been truly by myself in a while, and that can only lead to thinking, which is not good in my current situation. I bet Mother is drinking coffee right now. I bet Logan is at training. My heart breaks in two, and I need to get busy. I'm about to get up and go to the garden when the man walks in, carrying a cup of coffee along with some food. Thank goodness. At least, I can concentrate on eating.

It seems silly for me to be sitting in here by myself and having people wait on me, so I devour my food quickly, wanting to leave. As I get up to carry my dishes back, the gentleman appears.

He shakes his gray head. "Please, leave it on the table. We will clean it up momentarily."

Sighing, I head outside. It's a beautiful day, but for some odd reason, the garden isn't calling my name. I walk around the mansion and find that I've made my way down to the stables. Once I get close to the gate, the stallion from the other day is standing out there in the middle of the field, watching me. He's completely gorgeous and doesn't appear menacing at all. Why would they say such a thing about him? I slowly climb over the gate – because, hey, that's what ladies do – but struggle in this horrible dress the seamstress has me in. I make it over and stroll slowly to him. His eyes appear curious, and I swear our souls are connecting.

As I approach him, I'm glad that Sam isn't here to mess this up again. The horse closes the final distance and nudges me with his nose. I move slowly to pet him, surprised that he's letting me. We stay like that for a few minutes, and then there is a commotion behind me.

"Miss, how'd you do that? He's never let anyone get close to him like that willingly," one of the stable boys calls out.

Alarm flashes in the horse's eyes, and he backs away and runs into a crop of trees.

No, I didn't want our time to end. However, I better answer these kids so I don't appear rude.

Heading toward the gardens, I call over my shoulder. "Oh, I was just slow and non-threatening. It's nothing at all."

I wander over to the bench seat and make myself comfortable. These trees aren't nearly as big as the ones in my home kingdom, but they are still beautiful in their own way. The colors are so bright and dazzling, almost as if the jewels feed their palette.

Of course, my thoughts go back to home. My heart hurts when I think of Emerson and Nick. I hope he doesn't treat her like he did me. I can't believe I fell for all his words and charms. Did he ever truly love me or if I was just convenient? For some reason, I can't get the girl's words out of my head. *Don't mistake kindness for convenience.* Is that what I did?

If I were the Savior, would things have been different? Better? I would never let anyone be treated the way Logan and I were treated while growing up if I had that kind of power. How was I so stupid to think Nick would stand up for what is right and true? When it comes down to it, he won't make a better king than his father. A good king stands up for what he believes in and fights for what's right. I thought that was him, and it seems unfair and cruel that I was wrong.

Lydia and Hazel were there to save me, but how did they know? I've always known she knew more than she let on, but how is that possible? What am I missing? And, frankly, why would they save me? My white power intrigues her, but is that enough to risk their lives if the king were ever to find out?

Thinking about my dear, loyal brother, sweet, carefree Claire, and steadfast mother hurts most of all. Why would I pursue a relationship with Nick that obviously jeopardized them? Gosh, I can't believe how foolish I've been. If only I could go back in time and make better choices.

Movement to my right catches my eye, and my power flares.

Sam is standing there watching me.

"Hey, pretty girl. What are you doing? You seem awfully down, which doesn't seem right with the beautiful scene I'm viewing."

I smile up at him, trying to hide my pain. I don't want him to feel like I'm only here because I have to be, even if it's true. I pat the place next to me, which causes that handsome smile to spread across his face.

"I thought you weren't going to be back until later?"

He frowns and huffs. "Well, it is almost five, but I did head back a little early. I needed to get away from there."

What happened today? I tilt my head. "Oh, why?"

He takes a deep breath and looks away, obviously not wanting to tell me what is going on.

Alarm flairs through me since this is exactly how Nick acted when he told me that he was engaged to my sister.

He reaches out and grabs my hand. "Calm down. It's nothing too terrible. It's just the Agrolon king is here, and so is Elizabeth."

"What? Why?" Do they know I'm here?

He gets up and leans back against one of the small trees. "Apparently, Pierce was right. They wanted to understand my quick departure and why I didn't attend the royal wedding as planned. This is a check-up visit to ensure we're still loyal."

What does this mean? Do I need to leave and go hide? "Oh, how long are they staying? Will they be coming here?"

He shakes his head in disgust. "Much to my chagrin, my mother asked Elizabeth if she would like to stay here at the mansion for a while. But as soon as she heard it wasn't a castle, she was out. This is one of the few times I'm thankful that she's so high maintenance."

I can't help but laugh, because we both know she's more than just high maintenance.

He grins knowingly.

"So, I'm safe?"

Sitting back down beside me, he strokes my arm. "Even if Elizabeth decided she wanted to come, I would have found a way to prevent it. You will always be safe with me."

I smile because he has become my comfort and safety. I'm not sure what I would ever have done without him. Why can't we work out? I care for him deeply. I lean against him, and he wraps his arm around my waist. "How long are they here for?"

He tilts my head up so I can see his wink. "Just a few more days, but don't worry. I'm all yours tomorrow. I made sure of it."

I smile and snuggle closer.

We stay outside for a little while longer, enjoying the day. Eventually, he tugs on my hand. "Hey, let's go eat. Supper should be ready and waiting for us, and I'm hungry. I skipped lunch so I could get back to you."

As expected, the dining table is ready, and we eat quickly. When we are done and walking out, he turns to me. "I'm so sorry, but I got up early and made the trip there and back in one day. I'm exhausted. I'm going to go to bed, but I was hoping we could get up and go swimming tomorrow. How does that sound?"

I haven't gone swimming in forever, but I don't have a bathing suit. "Uh, I would love to but don't have the appropriate attire."

He grins. "Don't you worry about it. You leave it to me. You'll have something delivered to your room first thing in the morning."

"Oh, Sam, no, I can't do that. You've already done so much, and I'm not doing anything to help you," I start, but he silences me with a chaste kiss.

His gaze softens and he brushes my chin. "You being here means more to me than you could ever know. You will be mine, Ari, and I take care of what is mine. I'll see you in the morning, so plan on getting soaked."

I head to my room and get ready for bed. I'm exhausted, too, so I lay down and go straight to sleep.

⚅⚄⚅

I am floating again in the forest. Luckily, it doesn't take as long to acclimate as the first time. It's a rush, because it seems as though I'm flying through the woods. I end up at the lake by the cave once again. However, this time, Owen is standing there alone.

He's sitting down by the water with his head in his hands. "Why can't I get you out of my head? You were only here for a few minutes. I don't need these distractions. I have a kingdom to lead… or, at least, what once was a kingdom." He continues mumbling, but I can't make out what he's saying.

His sister walks into the moonlight and stands behind him.

"What ya' doin' out here, Owen?"

I can tell he's startled only because I can see his face. However, other than that split-second expression, he doesn't let on that he didn't know she was there.

He grins. "You know, contemplating life and looking for unicorns."

She moves beside him and lightly kicks his arm. "Yeah, don't make fun of my childhood dreams. Unicorns are awesome and could totally kick your ass while pooping rainbows."

He laughs, and I'm surprised at how genuine it sounds. There isn't any false pretense in it, and it's the most attractive sound that I've ever heard. He really is gorgeous.

She cuts her eyes over to him. "You've been acting weird the past few days, ever since that girl stumbled upon us."

He grunts and doesn't say anything.

She sits beside him and leans into his side. "Well, your silence speaks volumes. Do you think she threatens us?"

He turns his head and squints at her. "No, not at all. You know that."

She puts her hand on the ground behind her, leaning back and looking at the moon. "Then, what is it?"

He's quiet and looks at where I am.

Can he see me, too? I'm about to move, but he glances away.

He puts his hands over his face. "I don't know, Mer. I can't get her out of my head."

My heart pounds at this declaration. Why am I here in mind, and why can't he get me out of his head? This is not normal.

She sits back up and moves his hands away from his face. "She has a pure heart, Owen. You're right. She doesn't threaten us, but she's foolish. She's extremely naive and has a lot of learning to go through. However, she is powerful, and her power is still growing. I've never felt that kind of power before, even from Mother."

He closes his eyes, and my heart breaks. I want to comfort him.

"Mer, you have no idea. You should have felt the magic of our blood oath. She... it took my breath away."

Mer laughs. "You've got the hots for her."

His face turns to stone. "She was gorgeous, but that doesn't matter. She's an outsider and can't be trusted. Even the pure of heart can accidentally hurt you."

At that, I am tugged back to my body as if his last statement is a warning.

Chapter Eight

I wake up to my power pulsing inside me, and I realize that I haven't used it in days. Lydia had warned me that, as my power increases, I need to deplete it regularly, so my body has time to adjust. I glance at the time and realize it's slightly before dawn and that, if I hurry, I can use some of it before Sam arrives.

After quickly changing into one of those horrid dresses, I sneak out the door that leads me to the gardens. I hurry, walking past the stables and into the trees that are several yards away. Looking around, trying to figure out what to do, I decide that it really doesn't matter. I just need to expel enough to make it more manageable for the day.

I find a branch that has fallen and reach to grab it. I hold it up and use my power to light it, and the whole thing blazes in my hand. My instinct is to drop it, but, to my horror, I realize it's not burning me. It's as if my whole hand is on fire.

Instinctively, I conjure water and soak my whole hand along with the branch. What the hell just happened? That can't be normal. I close my eyes and concentrate on keeping the queasy feeling at bay. After several deep breaths, I open my eyes to check my hand. What in Knova? My skin is perfectly smooth. How is that possible? Every time I've lit something, it was just the object. How did I manage to light the branch and my hand, but not mar my skin?

Yeah, I don't think I should be lighting anything else up today. Oh, yes. I remember the misting technique Lydia taught me and begin imagining my power evaporating from me. It takes a lot longer than I expect to get enough of it out to make me feel normal. I can't go that long without using my power again. It's getting way too strong for that.

I hurry back to my room and notice a guard making the rounds. Right when he turns his head to look my way, I blast my power and send a strong gust of wind out, which knocks him off his feet.

He lands on his bottom. "What the hell?"

I make my escape into my room.

When I make it to the safety of my room, I quietly shut the door and lean back against it. What is going on with me? Too much stuff is changing again, but I don't have anyone here to help or confide in like I did back home.

I'm on the verge of tears, because everything is spiraling out of control again. I have no home, no family, and no guidance for my crazy powers. Tears pour from my eyes, and then there is a knock at my door. I take a deep breath and head over to open the door. My eyes widen.

Why is Pierce here? He glances down the hallway before sliding into the room and shutting the door.

What is he doing? I can't stay in here alone with him.

He glances at me. "Calm down. I'm here to help you."

How does he know I need help? "What do you mean? What are you talking about?"

"You need to be more careful. Luckily, I'm the only one who noticed your adventure. I followed you and saw everything." He pauses, watching my reaction.

"Oh, great. So, are you here to blackmail me, or are you warning me that you're going to tell the king and queen?"

His eyes widen, and he raises his hands in surrender. "No, no, nothing like that. Look, I don't want them to find out. Between you and me, they aren't much better than King Percy. They are conniving opportunists. However, up until now, they have sheltered the prince."

Okay, this is surprising. "What? Everyone seems to love Sam."

"Yes, he's been protected, but he won't be much longer. Look, you can't let him know what you can do. They will try to use you against your kingdom. Granted, right now, the queen thinks you're dead, but let's be frank. How long do you think that will last?"

Could I really ruin that? "But they are allies. They can't go back on their word."

He shakes his head, clearly disappointed. "Don't be so naive. Betrayal happens all the time, especially when power comes into play. The best thing you can do is stay as low key as possible. That way, when the queen finds out, you won't be used as a pawn. She won't kill you, because Sam would rebel. You're safe, and our kingdom is safe, as long as you keep what you're doing hidden. Do you understand?"

I take a deep breath, absorbing all this information. Why am I so powerful? I'm not the Savior, but yet, I can do things that haven't been done in years. I bite my lip and nod. I hadn't planned on anyone knowing anyway.

His shoulders seem to lower and some worriy leaves his face. "Okay, good. Now, no more using your powers."

That can't happen. I already lit my hand on fire because of that. "That's impossible. That's why I snuck out this morning. I haven't used it for several days, and the longer I hold off, the more uncontrollable it is. I need to be depleting it every day since it's continuing to grow."

This bit of news clearly disappoints him. He grunts and rubs his hands down his face. "Okay, I will sneak out with you at night when it's completely dark. I'll stay here all the time instead of returning to the palace. I'll figure out something to explain my absence at the palace with the queen. I can pick you up outside your door when everyone is asleep. I'll knock very lightly so you'll need to listen."

I can't ask to do that. "No, I can go by myself. I don't need to bother you."

His golden eyes capture mine. "Oh, I'm coming. I followed you the whole time, and you were completely clueless. I'm going to ensure you're safe and not followed. Do you need to go now?"

I focus on my power, checking to see if it's still too strong. "No, I should be good, and honestly, I'm exhausted after my early morning excursion. Let's start tomorrow night."

"All right, I'll be ready." He walks out the back door as quiet as a mouse.

No wonder I couldn't hear him. Once again, I'm in a situation I have no control over. However, at least someone knows, and I can somewhat confide in him. It's odd, though. He always seems to just materialize.

As soon as he's gone, there is a knock at my door, and I'm

tempted not to answer it. I've had enough happen for the day, and it's only nine in the morning.

"Miss, I'm here to deliver your swimsuit," a voice calls out.

I forgot that Sam said he'd get someone to deliver my bathing suit. I hurry to the door and open it up halfway. Emily is standing there with a smile and hands it to me. "Do you need any help?"

"Oh, no. Thank you so much, Emily. I can take it from here." I grab the bathing suit and smile at her. "I appreciate you bringing it to me."

She curtseys and lowers her head. "No problem. Let me know if you need anything else."

I close the door and walk back to the bed to examine the modest, one-piece, emerald-hued bathing suit she delivered. I lay it down on the bed, and then there is another knock at my door. Ugh, I just wanted another ten minutes of sleep.

"Ari, are you there?" Sam calls out.

I guess there is no nap in the near future. It's time to go swimming. "Hold on, let me change into my bathing suit. I'll be out in a few minutes."

"Okay, that's fine. Just wanted to make sure you're awake. How about we meet in the dining hall so we can eat breakfast before we head out?"

Yes, food would be great, especially this morning. "That sounds great. I'm actually starving this morning. I'll be there soon."

I pull off the hideous dress and quickly put on the one-piece. Luckily, it fits perfectly. I put my dress back on over it to wear until we get there. When I fix my hair, I make sure all the strands are in place and put a little make-up on to cover the dark circles under my eyes.

Once I'm ready, I rush to the dining table and sit next to Sam, finding my plate is already there waiting for me. Sam grins at me and picks his fork up to begin eating. "Oh, you didn't have to wait for me."

He winks, his brown eyes shining. "Of course, I did, pretty girl. You're the best part of the experience. I can't start without you."

How am I the best part of the meal? He's the only Royal besides Nick who hasn't viewed me as a nuisance. My tummy rumbles, and I scarf down my food. The corner of Sam's mouth are raised as if he's trying not to laugh. "You sure weren't kidding about starving this morning."

I stick my tongue out at him even though I have a mouth full of food, and he laugh hard. "I love how you don't try to impress me. Please, don't ever change."

Finally, someone accepts me for me. Smiling, we both quickly finish so we can start the day.

We head to the stables, saddle some horses, and take off for our trip. He takes me to a pond that isn't too far from the mansion but a good distance away from the villagers. It's extremely gorgeous. There is a grassy embankment that slopes down to the pond. There are a few sparse trees surrounding it, but overall, it's wide open, and the water is the color of the sky. It's so clear that I can see all the little fish swimming around in it.

Sam motions me over with his hands. "Come on, let's go for a dip. Don't worry, we will have this place all to ourselves. It's on the mansion property, and it's unknown by the villagers."

Even if that's the case, no one besides my brother and mother has ever seen me in a bathing suit. Honestly, it's been over eight years since they have. When the beatings from the king started leaving scars, I stopped swimming and would just put my feet in the water.

It's strange that when I reached Enlightenment at eighteen that they all physically vanished. However, the emotional trauma still hangs around, so getting back in a bathing suit is hard. But, I totally have this. So, I take off my dress as quickly as possible and jump in the water.

Sam laughs. "A little eager, are we?"

I give him a warning glare, and he laughs more. He quickly gets down to his swim trunks and joins me in the water. We float around and just enjoy being lazy. Sam swims over to me and wraps his arms around my waist. His arms always offer me comfort and safety, so I snuggle closer to him.

He leans back slightly and puts one of his fingers under my chin, tilting my head up so he can gaze into my eyes. "Ari, I know you said you need time, but I love you. I'll do everything to make you happy. Please, will you give us a chance? That's all I'm asking."

Here is this handsome, nice, caring man asking for a chance. Why can't I give him that? If that's what he wants, he deserves to have it. He saved me, after all, and has proven his loyalty. I mean, it took years for my feelings to grow so strong for Nick, so it makes sense that it would be the same with Sam. Yes, Owen made an immediate impact on me, but he's made it clear that he doesn't like me and that I'm not to be trusted. My mother always said that true love takes time, and I do already care for Sam deeply.

I glance back, meeting his eyes. "Okay, I can give us a chance."

He smiles brightly, and I breathe out in relief. I made him happy, which is what he truly deserves. I can do this. I can start fresh. He bends down and kisses me. I return the kiss, but it doesn't seem right. I wait a little longer, because I don't want to hurt him, and then crawl out of the water to lie out in the sun on a blanket.

I glance over and find Sam watching me. He grins. "You're really beautiful. Do you know that?"

He means to be tender, but I never know how to react to those types of compliments. Before him, I never really had those. Thunder rumbles, and I look up and notice some dark clouds are rolling in.

I sit up. "We better get going. A storm is heading our way."

He glances up and nods, getting out of the water. "I guess so. Want to go back and play checkers?"

A game sounds like fun. I get up and slip my dress back on. "You're on."

He frowns and clutches his chest. "I'm sure going to miss that view."

I roll my eyes and throw his clothes at him.

He grabs them, holding them away from his body. "Hey, you're going to get them wet." He puts the clothes down and reaches for his towel.

I'm enjoying this day and don't want it to end, but at least we have checkers. We quickly get moving and reach the house just as the rain comes pouring down. We rush in, trying to get out of the rain, laughing the entire way. "Good thing you didn't let your clothes get wet," I giggle.

He pulls me toward him. "Hey, be nice." He kisses my lips, and once again, I want to pull away. The last thing I want to do is hurt him, especially after I promised to give him a chance, so I lightly kiss him back.

I pull away and raise an eyebrow. "What about that game of checkers."

He groans. "Ari, you're going to kill me. Fine, let's go make you happy, pretty girl."

He takes me into a room I've never been in before that is loaded with games and has a table and chairs in the center. It looks similar to the library, only with games stacked upon one another.

I turn around, taking in the whole room. "Whoa, what is this?"

Sam looks around and purses his lips. "My father takes his games seriously. A lot of these are strategic games he is using for battle training. I have no clue why. I mean, Crealon is trying to rise, but now that we are aligned with Agrolon, and the Savior is part of their family, there is no way a war will actually take place. They'd be stupid to try, but father needed to work on it in case it all didn't work out this way, I guess. So, he made this room for his 'studies'."

Why in Knova would his father encourage that if he was truly satisfied with their place? They have hopes of still coming out on top. This proves some of what Pierce was talking about earlier.

Sam pulls out checkers and sets it out on the table. We play the game for a while, and he gets frustrated when I win the majority of the time. He looks at me dejectedly. "Don't ever tell my father what has just happened. He'll say I didn't practice enough growing up."

I almost laugh but stop short. "How would I ever have the chance? Your parents think I'm dead."

Sam sobers up. "Oh, Ari, we will tell them. How many

times do I have to say that you will be mine? I just need to wait until Elizabeth is out of our hair."

I nod, wanting to believe him, but Nick's false promises ring loud in my ears. What is wrong with me? Of course, Sam isn't anything like Nick. Right? I'm not making the same mistake again, am I? My skin crawls. Sam is taking in everything, and the displeasure is apparent on his face.

"You're thinking about him, aren't you? You think I'd do the same thing to you?" he growls.

Guilt must be showing, because anger is apparent in his eyes. He's never been angry with me, and I'm not sure how to react. He jumps up from the table and walks over to me. His face reddening, he presses, "Aren't you?"

I want to lie, but I can't. I never want to be purposely untruthful to him. He deserves better than that. "Yes, I'm so sorry."

"I'm not him. Do you know how much that hurts? All I've done is try to protect and take care of you. I caused strife with my parents for abandoning the Agrolon's wedding to get you to safety, and at the first opportunity, you want to think poorly of me." His voice grows louder. "Would you rather me go there now and announce it, so Elizabeth can run home to her father and tell him that you're alive, and my kingdom can be labeled a traitor? Is that what you want, Ari?"

My heart races in fear. I've never seen Sam like this, and honestly, I'm not sure what to do. He's so angry that I can see a vein pop up between his normal, comforting brown eyes. I just want to disappear and run to my room. Tears fill my eyes. "No, of course not. I didn't mean to compare you to Nick. Of course, you aren't him. I know you've risked a lot for me, and I'm forever thankful. I am so, so sorry."

Bang. Bang. Someone is knocking loudly on the door.

Sam closes his eyes and puts his hand on his forehead. "Who is it?"

"It's Pierce, my Prince. The staff asked me to let you know that dinner is ready."

Sam's face reddens. "Tell them we'll be there in a second."

This is my time to get out of this uncomfortable situation. I'm not missing it. "I'm ready now."

Sam shoots daggers my way, and I cringe.

The door opens, and Pierce walks into the room. Pierce glances at me, and it's obvious that he knew something was going on behind these doors. How does he always seem to know these things?

Sam glares at my knight in shining armor. "Pierce, I told you we would be there in a minute. Why are you here?"

Pierce maintains an indifferent face and simply answers him. "Because Ariah said she was ready. I thought I could accompany you all."

Sam startles and scowls at Pierce. "Why in Knova would you think you should accompany us? You aren't allowed to dine with us."

Oh, no. I'm getting Pierce in trouble. I reach out, inter-locking my arm with Sam's. "I'm starving, and I'm sure Pierce just meant walk with us to the dining room. Can we please eat? It's been a long day."

Sam glances down at our interlocked arms, and some of his anger seems to dissipate. He gives me a tight grin. "Of course. I'm sorry. I wasn't thinking."

Pierce speaks in a whisper, "Obviously."

I cringe, waiting for Sam to implode.

He must not have heard, because his eyes are still firmly on me.

He looks at me. "Come on, pretty girl. Let's go get you something to eat."

I don't look him in the eyes but nod. I really want this evening to just be over.

The three of us head to the dining hall, and right before Pierce splits off to go to the help's kitchen, he looks at Sam. "Remember, my Prince, your mother is requesting your presence tomorrow morning. Apparently, Princess Elizabeth will be returning to her kingdom."

Sam nods and continues on course. We sit down for dinner, and it's oddly quiet. There is tension between us, and I just need some space to clear my head.

Thankfully, it's a quick meal. However, Sam is trying to linger. How can I get to my room? I take a deep breath and glance up at him. "I'm sorry, but I'm exhausted. I couldn't sleep well last night, and then we had such a lovely day. Do you mind if I go on to bed?"

He frowns and fidgets in his seat. "Yes, I need to get some rest as well. I'll be back tomorrow evening, and maybe we can spend some time together?"

His words are so unsure. I hate that I make him feel this way, but I truly didn't mean to. I'm not sure what to do. I don't like how things are changing between us.

I give him a small grin. "Of course, I'd love to."

He rises to walk me to my room, but thankfully, Pierce enters the room. "Sir, I hate to bother you, but I need your assistance with something."

Sam is clearly not happy with the interruption, but I jump at this opportunity. "Oh, it's okay, Sam. I can find my way to my room. You go take care of your kingdom."

I peck him on the cheek quickly and walk out the door before he can figure out a way to join me.

When I get to my room, I shut the door and release the breath I've been holding. I don't know what's going on between Sam and me, but it doesn't seem to be good. However, I need to fix it. I have nowhere else to go. Times like this make me miss my mother even more. I would really appreciate words of wisdom from her.

Chapter Nine

So happy to have the morning to myself, I crawl out of bed more ready to tackle the day than I have been in a while. I need time to figure out how to fix this tension between Sam and me, and it'll be easier to come up with something if he isn't sitting right next to me.

I get ready and walk to the dining hall to eat, now aware to never make the mistake of walking into the kitchen again. The older gentleman quickly appears with a smile on his face and my coffee in hand. "Morning, miss. How are you this beautiful morning?"

I smile at him. "I'm doing well. How are you?"

He grimaces. "Doing as well as I can be at this dreadful age. Here is your coffee. I'll go grab your breakfast right now."

I take a sip of my coffee and breathe in the aroma. True to his word, he's already walking back with my food. "Thanks." I smile at him and dig right in.

As soon as I'm through, I get up and head to the stables. I'm wondering if my stallion friend is around. To my delight,

JEN L. GREY

he's standing where I usually find him. "Hey, boy. I'm sure glad to see you," I coo at him, heading slowly toward him. He watches me as I get close, stomping impatiently. I reach him and pet his forehead. He neighs, and I get closer. We stay like this for a little while, until eventually, I pull away. I need to move around and get some fresh air, so I decide to take a walk through the woods, and the horse follows behind me.

I take a very long walk and come to the pond Sam and I swam in the day before. Sitting on the embankment, I think of our time here. We had so much fun. I wish it hadn't started raining. Maybe the weird tension between us wouldn't have happened. It has something to do with Nick, but what is triggering all this? I'm here with him, obviously, and Nick is married for goodness sake. But why are my feelings about Sam so confusing? I enjoy his company and care for him, but recently, his kisses have begun to bother me and just don't feel right. At the palace back home, they were pleasant. Even the first night in the tent, when things were going too far, it didn't feel wrong then. My feelings changed the evening after I met Owen, but that can't be the reason. That's just a crazy coincidence.

The stallion emerges from the tree line it had stopped at. He lays down next to me, and I lean into him.

His presence is comforting, and I stroke the back of his head. "Since we are getting to be friends, you need a name. Let's see, you're grey, and people think you are wild. Let's give you a warrior's name. Oh, I'll call you Ares."

He snorts, so I take that as agreement. We stay there for a while until I realize that the sun is about to set. How did I lose track of time like that? I jump up, hurrying to get back. Ares runs in front of me and stomps just like earlier. I have no clue what he wants, but I decide to try riding him. I'd get there a lot faster with him carrying me.

When I get on his back, he's fine with it. He immediately takes off, almost like he can sense my alarm. As the stables come into view, Sam is one of the first things in sight. He's on a horse, and yelling, but I can't make out what he's saying. Someone points in my direction, and he takes off over to me.

When he gets close, I can see panic all over his face. His usually neat brown hair is in crazy spikes, his clothes are rumpled, and his cheeks are red. "Thank goodness, you're okay, Ari. I've been worried sick. Where have you been, and how in Knova did you get that horse to let you ride?"

I dismount off the horse, and Sam follows my lead. He grabs my hand and cups my cheek with his free hand. "Don't ever scare me like that again. Seriously, where were you?"

"I'm so sorry. I had the morning to myself, so I went back to the pond from yesterday. I enjoyed it there and apparently lost track of time." I expect this to anger him, and I wait for the backlash.

However, his worried expression morphs into a huge smile, which throws me off kilter. "No, it's okay. Just, do you mind telling someone next time you go off alone? I was worried something happened to you," he asks, kindly.

I don't know why he isn't angry, but I'm not chancing it again. "Yes, I promise to let someone know. I truly planned on being back here before you got home so I didn't worry you. I don't know what happened."

He pulls me into his arms and kisses my head. "Seriously, it's okay, and honestly, I came back earlier than expected. Let's go clean up and grab some dinner."

My heart calms down. Thank goodness, he's not angry. I was so afraid we would have another blow up like yesterday.

I turn to see Ares walking into the trees and continue my trek to the mansion.

I wash up in the bathroom and meet Sam in the dining hall. The room is darker than normal due to the candles that are lit everywhere. I'm confused and move to turn back around when Sam comes into the faint light.

He takes my hand and leads me to the table. "Hey, pretty girl. I was hoping we could have our dinner by candlelight. Make it a little more special tonight."

We sit down, and after I take my first bite of food, I take several more bites quickly. Oh my goodness, the food is better than normal. It doesn't take long before my plate is clear, my nerves getting the best of me.

When Sam finally gets done, he looks over at me and takes my hand. "So, I talked to Mother today. As soon as Elizabeth left, I told her that you are staying here with me and that I intend to make you mine in all ways."

My breath gets caught up my throat. Why would he tell his mother?

"Sam, do you think that was the best thing? I mean, doesn't that put her in a bad situation?"

Sam shakes his head. "Well, I had to tell her, Ari. I know this makes things strange and complicated, and I may have to travel to Agrolon without you, but you can live here in the mansion with me."

At that, he drops down before me on one knee. My heart seems to have stopped beating. He reaches into his pocket and pulls out the most beautiful emerald ring I have ever seen. Even though the room is dark, the jewel still shines brightly, almost as if it's daring the shadows to try to dim the gem's brilliance. Sam looks into my eyes and holds the ring out to my finger. "Ari, I love you with my whole soul. Will you please be my bride?"

I'm not sure what to do or say. I mean, really, what option do I have? I can't go home, and I do care for Sam. However, something is holding me back. Tears fill my eyes, and I take a shuddering breath. "Oh, Sam, I want to say yes, but I can't. I told you I needed time, and just yesterday you asked me to give us a chance. This is moving too fast for me. I'm so sorry, but the answer is no at this time. If I did, it wouldn't be for the right reasons."

I'm so afraid that I've upset him, and he slowly sits back down in his chair. He has a pained expression on his face, and he sets the ring gently on the table. The silence is deafening, and my palms are growing sweaty. After several long moments, he looks over at me and takes my hand.

"I'm so sorry, Ari. You're right." He chuckles, harshly. "I did just ask you to take a chance on us yesterday. It's just… I want you to know how serious I am about us. Seeing you question my sincerity yesterday hurt deeply. We can take it as slow as you need. I'll wait forever for you."

He lifts me up from my seat and kisses my lips quickly, then he smiles and takes my hand. We head out to the gardens and lay side by side on the ground, looking up at the stars and moon. He reaches out and interlocks our fingers. It's a beautiful night, and my power hums inside me. It's getting strong again, but luckily, I have my excursion with Pierce tonight, so I should be able to rein it back in.

Thinking of my power brings the queen to mind. "So, what exactly did you tell your mother?"

Sam stiffens. "Well, I told her you are here and that I intend to make you mine."

Yeah, I'm sure she just let that drop. "How did she react?"

He plays with my fingers. "Well, she wasn't thrilled, to be honest. However, with time, she'll come to accept my decision."

My heart races and my breath quickens. Of course, she isn't happy. I'm the outcast from Agrolon. "Okay, that was a nice answer. Now, tell me her real reaction."

Rubbing the side of his face, he lets out a heavy sigh. "Well, she said that you are not for me. But, she'll come around. She always does." He looks at me and winks.

This isn't great and it's not a game, but I drop it. I'm sure she said more, and I can only imagine what she's saying now. However, I am glad that Sam took my rejection so well earlier. Maybe we are back on course. We spend the rest of the night enjoying each other's company until I get up, explaining that I'm ready for bed.

He escorts me to my room, and when we reach my door, he caresses my cheek with the palm of his hand. He kisses my lips lightly, and I turn and walk in, shutting the door. I crawl into bed and wait for Pierce.

◈

A quiet knock wakes me from my slumber. Apparently, I dozed off while waiting for Pierce. I quickly open the door, and he immediately walks in.

He touches my shoulder. "Are you okay?"

I rub my eyes. "Yes, sorry. I must have fallen asleep, but I'm ready. My power is already brimming."

He heads to the back terrace, quietly opening the door. He disappears for a minute but comes back. "Be quiet and listen to everything I say."

I nod and follow behind him. After a few minutes, we are at the stables and heading through the trees out to the clearing. As soon as we get through the clearing, I imagine my power pouring out of my skin. I feel it flowing out of me in huge waves.

I hear a clear intake of air.

Looking for the noise, I find Pierce staring at me in wonder.

When I take inventory of myself, I realize that my power is pouring from my body out into the air, almost like a dense fog. I'm not sure what else to do, because it doesn't seem to have depleted much, and I can't stop it.

After a short time, the power is getting thicker and thicker in the air. Pierce is continually moving back, trying not to get caught up in it. I pull water from the air, but it doesn't stop the fog. It keeps getting denser. I then make the air around us swirl and push the fog away, but it still rolls off me.

Desperate, I decide to push the power into the ground instead of the air. Instead of the power rolling off me, I imagine it traveling down my feet and into the ground. As soon as it seeps into the ground, the grass grows under my feet and around me, and the trees near me grow bigger and healthier. My power seems to be depleting, so I pour more into the soil.

After all this, my power isn't thrumming anymore and is more of a weak pulse inside of me. I open my eyes. What in Knova happened? The trees are now huge, almost the same size as the trees back home. The grass is a healthier shade of green and not the usual brownish-green. There are small, baby trees growing, and flowers are blooming like crazy.

Pierce walks up, his eyes wide. "I have never seen

someone do something so amazing. You've revived this part of our kingdom. I bet we could plant something here and it would actually grow."

Feeling uncomfortable under his gaze, I start the trek back to the mansion. Before I get far, he puts his hand on my shoulder and lightly turns me around.

He looks into my eyes before telling me sincerely, "Be careful with Sam. Things are changing. I don't think I need to tell you that people may hurt you unintentionally."

His words startle me. Owen had said something similar the night I was... watching. Stalking is by choice, right? So, since I have no control over it, we'll call it watching. A lot less creepy that way.

I shake my head and make my way back to my bed.

Chapter Ten

The next morning, I'm out of bed before sunrise. I tossed and turned all night, dreaming crazy things. You'd think a room this beautiful would keep the nightmares at bay.

My dream seemed so real. I was being chased, but I'm not sure why. It almost seems as if my time is running out, but for what?

I quickly change, needing a strong cup of coffee. As soon as I'm sitting down in the dining hall, the older gentleman is bringing the goods. I take a large sip and grin. "You, kind sir, are my knight in shining armor."

He chuckles. "I haven't been called that in a long time."

Sam comes through the door, holding a hand over his heart. "Uh oh, do I have competition now?"

I grin, so thankful that things haven't changed between us like I had been afraid of. "Maybe. He makes a mean cup of coffee."

The older man comes back in with breakfast, and Sam looks over at me. "Why don't we go into town?"

"I don't think that would be a very wise idea, my son," a voice interjects.

Much to my horror, Sam's mother is standing right at the dining room door. Sam is out of his chair in an instant.

Sam stands in front of me. "Mother, what are you doing here?"

Her eyes narrow in my direction. "Trying to figure out what the hell you are doing."

He folds his arms across his chest. "Spending time with the woman I love."

Her eyes widen in shock, but she quickly regains composure. "Oh, dear goodness. You really are stupid. I gave you so much leeway, hoping that when the time came you'd finally step up."

His face reddens and he glares at her. "I am not stupid, Mother."

His mother just looks at him in disgust, and then, her eyes are back on me.

A few moments later, Pierce walks in with a very solemn face.

She turns to him. "Please, bring all my stuff in. I'll stay in the guest room in the east wing. I assume she has the one in the west end."

Pierce nods and glances at me quickly. As soon as he's left, Sam speaks up. "You never stay here."

She focuses her attention back to her son. "I know, but I think it's time I stay and visit for a while."

She turns and walks out of the room, leaving the tension behind. Sam winces and turns to me. "I am so sorry. I had no clue she'd come here and act like that. Come on, let's go into town."

I shake my head. "No, she's already upset, and I don't

think it's wise to push her any further. How about we go swimming instead?" His face lights up at the suggestion. I smile at his enthusiasm, and we both head to our bedrooms to change. I quickly change into a black one-piece bathing suit, throwing my clothes back on over the top of it, and grab a towel. By the time I have my long, dark red hair tied in a bun, Sam is back and knocking on my door.

When he sees me, his face turns into a grin, and he grabs my towel, leading us down to the stables. As soon as we make it to the gates, Ares comes out of the trees, heading in my direction. Sam stands there with his mouth hanging open as the stallion comes right up to me. I reach out and pet him, and he stomps.

I walk over to him, about to mount, when Sam opens his mouth to speak.

I know exactly what he's going to say, so I go ahead and get on Ares' back, effectively cutting him off. Sam hurries to get on his horse, and for once, Ares is content waiting.

Soon, we are all off and heading toward the swimming hole. Ares and I run the entire way, and it's exhilarating. We reach the water before Sam and his mare. I slide off Ares and go to sit on the embankment. A short time later, Sam catches up.

He sits beside me and glances back at Ares. "What in Knova! That horse is fast, and he's letting you ride him. I guess I shouldn't be surprised by this. You are truly an amazing woman." He pulls me close and kisses my lips. "It feels like forever since we've had time together like this."

I give him a tight grin. "I know. You've been very busy lately."

Sam looks at the sky. "Thank goodness, that witch... I mean, Elizabeth is gone. She was about to drive me crazy."

JEN L. GREY

I think he's not telling me the whole truth, but at this point, I don't want anything else to deal with. I stare out at the beautiful, clear water, and the sun is shining brightly without a single cloud in the sky. I lean my back against Sam's chest, and he wraps his arms around my waist. There is a faint breeze blowing, and the day is absolutely gorgeous.

He moves his hands up to rub my shoulders. "Hey, did you notice that very healthy patch of land we went through to get here? It's like something revived that little section."

I cringe, wishing he hadn't noticed.

He takes my silence as an answer. "It was incredible, Ari. You'll have to see it when we get back. I'm not going to say anything to Mother yet, because who knows what caused it, but I'm hopeful that our country is going to rebound now."

I love how he cut off at now. He doesn't need to explain what he means, though, and the air fills with unease as I let his words sink in. Now that my sister is the princess and the Savior of the country.

I try to relax my body and enjoy this beautiful day. Luckily, he's smart enough to stop talking. We stay like this for a while until Sam stands up, pulling me to my feet. "Let's go swimming. We can lay around afterward when we need to dry off."

Laughing, I oblige. Soon, we are both in the water and having a good time. We swim for a while, and then Sam grabs me, pulling me into his arms. Our bodies are flush against one another, and before I realize what's happening, his lips are on mine. Our mouths collide, and our kisses become urgent. "Ari, I love you so damn much."

I want to stop him, but he's been so patient that I'm trying to enjoy it. However, when he presses his hips into my body, the whole situation doesn't seem right. I try to ignore the uneasy feeling, but then heat flares through my body, and I pull away from him, needing to escape his body heat. The water doesn't cool me either, and I almost lose my breath.

Sam grabs me pulling me toward the rocky shore. "Ari? Ari, are you okay?"

As soon as my feet touch the ground, I drag myself the rest of the way out of the water and onto the embankment, trying to catch my breath.

He moves beside me and touches my arm. "You're burning up again."

I whimper and scoot away from him. I hold my hands up, trying not to be mean.

"Please, give me a second. I don't know what's happening, but I'm cooling off. I just need a minute."

He nods, keeping a safe distance from me.

I take deep, steady breaths, trying to contain the lingering inferno within me. This feels similar to my power but different. Almost like a stronger power, but I don't know what's causing it or what it means. I sigh, wishing that Lydia was here with her riddles and games. At least, she was able to provide some type of guidance, even if it was a maze to figure out.

I lay back on the ground, closing my eyes and concentrating on the breeze. The air is clear out here and not metallic like in the city where all the mining takes place. Sometime later, the fire inside me fizzles, and I sit up under the watchful gaze of Sam.

I feel bad. His eyes are full of concern, but he keeps his distance, respecting my earlier wishes. "You okay now? Maybe we should take you to a healer."

Oh, no. I don't want to see a healer. I shake my head. "No,

I'm fine. I don't know what's going on, but I'm sure it will all level out."

He rubs the back of his head not happy. "Ari, I could feel the heat coming off of you. I almost let you go in the water, because you were so hot. Thank goodness, I was able to hold on."

Seeing that type of concern in his eyes alleviates some of my hesitancy I've built up with him. He truly cares for me, and I really do care deeply for him. He's protected me from day one, so why am I holding back from him?

Owen flashes in my mind. Why in Knova am I thinking of him at a time like this? I push his image away and try to focus back on Sam.

He walks toward me and helps me up. "We better get back. If you flare up like that again, I want to make sure we are home and not somewhere we could drown."

He kisses my lips, but the concern never leaves his face. Ares walks over to me and is a lot calmer than I've ever seen him. The whole way back to the mansion is at a slow pace, almost as if he knows my body can't handle the jarring.

Sam carries all of our things back to the house, and I realize as we walk inside that I'm still only wearing my bathing suit.

I never put my clothes back on, so all of the staff is seeing me in essentially my underwear. Oh, my goodness, I can't believe this is happening. I keep my eyes on the ground, hoping that it will make me invisible.

Sam opens my door and steps inside, dropping off my clothes and towel. "Hey, I bet a cool shower might do you good. Let me go start the water for you."

My heart warms at his consideration, and if I ever doubted he cared, all of that has been eliminated as of today.

When he comes out, he brushes his fingers along my arm.

Needing him to know how much I care for him, I stand on my tiptoes and kiss him deeply.

He groans in response and pulls me against him. My hands tangle in his hair, and he deepens the kiss even more. Our tongues collide, and he grips my waist with both hands before splaying his fingers and moving them up my body. Just when his fingers graze my rib cage, fire bursts from inside me again. He jumps back, giving me room. "What the hell? You're hot as fire again."

I don't understand why this keeps happening. It seems to happen each time Sam and I get too intimate.

He begins to move toward me but stops himself. "Why don't you go get under the water, and I'll meet you in the dining room."

I shake my head no, not wanting to be around his mother.

He smiles and soften his tone. "Hey, does a picnic sound good? We could eat in the garden."

I nod my head, thankful for the change in plans. His mother wouldn't dare eat out in the garden.

His eyes filled with love. "Okay, go relax, and I'll get everything ready. Don't rush. I'll wait on you."

"Thank you. I'll be there soon," I promise.

I walk into the bathroom and decide that a bath sounds better than a shower. I turn the water off and fill up the tub. I sit on the edge, waiting for the water to fill up, and throw some lavender soaps in. Once it is full enough, I slip out of my bathing suit and submerge myself.

Once I get settled in, I fall asleep.

☙❧

I'm flying through the woods again. Why does this keep happening? Soon, I'm coming to the village, only this time, I'm not by the cave or the pond. I'm in one of the houses built into the trees. It's very nice inside, with hardwood ceilings and floors. Everything is made out of wood, but the seats all have cushions, so they look comfortable to sit on. When I look around, Owen is lying on a couch, and his sister is beside him.

She's frantic and shaking him. "Owen, what's wrong? You're burning up."

He looks at her, but in a daze. "I'm not sure. It seems like something is not right, and I don't know how to fix it. I was wrong. She's the key."

As soon as I hear those words, I'm being pulled back out of the house and through the woods.

꧁꧂

I startle awake in the tub, breathing quickly. Why do I keep doing that? What's wrong with Owen? My necklace burns against my skin, and I realize it's been a while since it's done anything.

I submerge myself underwater, hoping that it will relieve the pain, but it does not help. I rise back up and take a deep breath, trying to be calm despite the searing pain. I try to remove it from my neck, but it won't come off.

Climbing out of the tub, I grab my towel to dry off then lay on the bed. After a long while, the burning ebbs, and I sigh in relief. This necklace seems to cause problems at the most inconvenient times.

I glance outside and realize that Sam is probably already

waiting for me in the garden. Jumping up, I pull on a light pink dress that cuts off at my knees and has an A-line top. I blow dry my hair and leave it straight, apply some lip gloss and mascara, and head out.

I walk out into the garden and find Sam sitting there on a blanket with the food already laid out. He smiles at me, but worry lines his face.

"Hey, pretty girl. What took so long? I was about to come in there but realized that might cause more of a scene."

I sit down beside him, and he moves closer to me, taking my hand. I look down and realize he brought some wine out and had candles placed strategically in the garden so we can easily see to eat since it's now dark. He is dressed in his emerald green shirt and tan dress pants.

"I'm sorry. I must have been wiped out by what happened earlier. I decided to take a bath and fell asleep in the bathtub. I'm so sorry. As soon as I woke up, I rushed here."

He leans over to kiss my lips. "Well, for rushing, you look absolutely stunning. However, I still miss your black hair."

I sure don't. "Well, it's kind of nice not to stick out amongst everyone."

Using his free hand, he plays with my hair. "You naturally stand apart from everyone. That's one of the things I love about you."

I close my eyes, enjoying his touch.

All too soon, he stops and grabs our plates. "We don't want the food to get cold."

That's quite true. The colder it gets, the worse its texture and taste is. It's best to eat it hot and fast.

We both eat, and then he pours us some wine to wash it all down. I've never really drunk alcohol before, but know not to drink it fast. I take a sip and am surprised by the sweet and delicious taste.

Sam chuckles. "It's good, isn't it?"

I lick my lips, trying not to miss a drop. "Yes, I've never had wine before. I always thought it would taste bitter."

He places a loose string of hair behind my ear. "Oh, there are some that do, but I figured this might be a good one for us. I've never seen you drink, so I figured we should start with something sweet."

I take another sip, enjoying the taste.

He raises an eyebrow. "You might want to slow down a little. Just because it's sweet doesn't mean it has any less of an effect."

The staff comes out and removes the dishes from our picnic.

When our blanket is clear, I lay back, setting my wine off to the side. The starry sky is once again beautiful, but there is a coolness in the air that I've never experienced before. I shiver, and of course, he notices.

He turns and cuddles with me.

I bury my face in his chest.

He buries his face in my hair, taking a deep breath. "The weather will be changing soon. Here, in the winter, it gets cold. Eventually, it will snow."

I can't wait to experience that. "Oh, I've never seen snow. It doesn't get cold enough back home for that." I cringe as soon as those words come out of my mouth, and he immediately stiffens.

After a few tense moments, he releases the breath he was holding. "Well, this is your home now, so you'll get to experience it."

I just nod, afraid to say anything else. For some reason, he always gets tense when I talk about Agrolon. Granted, I try not to think about it, because it's still way too painful.

After a few minutes, Sam pulls away from me so he can see my face. "Ari, I know we agreed to take things slow, but I want to give you something that shows my undying loyalty."

He reaches into his pocket and pulls out the same emerald ring he had proposed with. He takes my hand and flips it over. "I want you to keep this. When the time is right, just put it on your ring finger." He places it in my hand. "I don't want to pressure you, but I want you to know my intent and that my loyalty is to you."

This isn't right. He shouldn't give me this. I reach for his hand, trying to give it back. "No, Sam. I can't accept this."

He refuses to take it and cups my face with his hands. "Ari, you will be my bride, so this is yours. You just need to let me know when you're ready for that to happen."

Moving his hand back to mine, he closes my fingers around the ring. He really wants me to keep it. Why can't I just return his feelings? What is holding me back? He pulls me back snug against him, and we lay in silence.

Someone clears their throat, which makes me jerk back and turn around. His Mother is there and found us in a compromising position.

Sam huffs, and the disappointment is clear on his face. "Hello, Mother. Did you want to join us?"

I stand and fidget.

She cuts her eyes over to me. "Well, I couldn't believe that you would rather eat out here instead of with your own mother, but now I see why."

Of course she isn't going to make this easy on me. I can't believe I let my guard down knowing she was here as well.

Sam meets her gaze, not backing down. "Mother, we

came out here to get away from your snide remarks and innuendos."

She stares at me, and my skin crawls. She's beautiful and smart, calculating every move. I've never really been around her, so this is a new experience. She instantly reminds me of King Percy. How can that be when Sam doesn't seem to have a problem standing up for himself, unlike Nick?

She attempts to look apologetic, but her eyes tell the truth. "Sorry, dear. I didn't mean anything by it. I just was looking forward to knowing more about Miss Ariah here. It seems she makes quite the impression on most people."

I want to cower behind Sam, but that really isn't an option anymore. I step beside him, facing his mother. He tries to step back in front of me again, but I don't let him. I take a deep breath. "Sure, I'd love to get to know you."

She smiles, and my heart sinks.

I fell right into her trap, but what other option do I have?

She heads toward the mansion, but looks back. "Excellent. Let's all spend the day together tomorrow. We'll take a trip to the castle. It's about time Ariah gets to see where we live. Now that's settled, I think I'll turn in for the evening. Good night."

Sam is tense and not thrilled at all. "Ari, why'd you do that? You gave her exactly what she wanted."

I glance at my hands, avoiding his eyes. I really don't want another fight. "I know, but if we are truly going to have a future together, I have to deal with this all eventually, right?"

He smiles wide and looks at me with adoration. "Yes, we sure are."

He lowers his lips to mine and kisses me.

The unease returns, and Owen along with the burning flares through my skin and mind again. Not wanting to upset

Sam, I suck it in and deal with it. Our kiss ends, and the burning eases.

He pulls me close and walks me to my room. At my door, I lean back against it as he traps me with his body. He plays with my hair, and his eyes fill with concern again. "Ari, I love you. I know you're doing this for us, but if my mother gets to be too much, please, let me know."

I place my hand on his shoulder and cut my eyes up to him. "Sam, I'll be okay."

He kisses my lips and pulls away. "Please, go get some rest. Tomorrow will be a long day. Goodnight, pretty girl. I'll see you in the morning."

I close the door, and my necklace is warm. I quickly change and crawl into bed, falling asleep instantly.

Chapter Eleven

T he door opens, and the sound startles me awake. I hurry out of bed, not wanting to be left in a more compromising position. Who in Knova could be in my room at this hour? Someone moves closer toward me, and my power flares, erupting my hand in flames.

With the room lit, Pierce halts, looking at me in wonder. He shakes his head. "You're going to the castle tomorrow. We need to get you depleted tonight. You don't want to be having issues with control while there."

I nod and glance down. Crap, I'm in my pajamas. I extinguish the flames and grab some clothes, running into the bathroom to change. When I emerge, some lights have been turned on.

Pierce looks apologetic. "I'm so sorry, Ari. I didn't think this through. I was just focused on you being able to use your power tonight."

I give him a small smile, trying to reassure him. "It's okay. I overreacted. Let's go."

He shakes his head, then moves to the door and outside.

He wants to drop this conversation as desperately as I do. We quickly make our way through the fields and come upon our training spot.

Since my power isn't completely overwhelming me yet, I focus on some training exercises that Lydia had me do back at the Pearson house. I work on all the elements and find that I can control them even better than I used to. Wondering if I can make the plants grow again, I focus on sending my power down into the soil like I did the other night. The grass, flowers, and plants immediately grow and bloom again. The grass turns an even deeper green color, and the flowers bloom like crazy. I'm lost in the moment when Pierce clears his throat.

I'm broken out of my stupor and look over at him. "Let's not go too crazy. People will notice, Ari."

Oh, I didn't think of that. "You're right, sorry."

He looks around, keeping an eye on the whole area. "Are you ready to head back?"

I yawn and stretch. "Yes, I'm tired. I think I've drained myself enough for the next couple of days."

We walk back, and I jump back in bed. Sleep once again takes me.

⚜

I wake up, but once again, I'm not in physical form. This time, I'm not in the dense forest like all the other instances. I'm actually back at the Pearson house, and Lydia is standing there, looking right at me. I'm surprised to see her but also startled at how the forest around the house seems to be turning brown. How is that possible? It's always been green and vibrant here.

Lydia smiles, her red lips contradicting with her white teeth. "Hello, dear. How are you?"

This is so weird. How is this possible? "What? You can see me?"

She grins at me. "Yes, of course, I can see you. I called you here. Don't you remember that I promised I'd be here when needed?"

"Lydia, how is this possible?"

Her face falls, and her eyes fill with sadness. "Time will tell all. But, right now, we need to talk about your immediate future. Get ready to run, for Sam won't be able to change fate. Nick's decisions set the course in motion."

I'm so tired of riddles. Can I not once get a freaking answer? "What are you talking about? Emerson is the Savior. Her fate is set. Why are you focusing on me?"

She reaches out and touches my face with tenderness. "Oh, Ari. I'm sorry, but you still have a ways to go to be what is needed. All will be revealed in time. Be strong, and remember that people have your back, even if it doesn't appear that way. You are strong and can stand on your own. Follow the key, for it won't lead you astray. You must go now, but we will meet again soon." She kisses my forehead and then I'm sucked back into my body.

Mornings when I wake up and have to rush usually wind up not being good. So, it's only fitting that this day begins that way. I'm running late to meet up with Sam's mother, and all too soon, there is a knock at my door.

I still need more time. "One minute."

I pull my hair up into a twist and actually seek out one of the nicest dresses in the closet. If we are going to the palace, I better look the part. His mother is already judging everything I do. I wish my own mother was here to apply my makeup. It takes me three times longer than it would her. I take one last look in the mirror before opening the door.

I'm wearing an elegant emerald green dress that is draped with straps in a V-neckline. It's long, and I worry about moving around easily, but I really need to dress the part. I am wearing tan eyeshadow, eyeliner, and mascara, and my lips are painted a deep pink. My necklace is hidden in my dress once again.

Sam is leaning back against the wall, waiting for me. I shut the door behind me, and he just stares. "You always seem to light up the room, especially in my kingdom's color."

I already don't feel comfortable in dresses and to add his remarks on top makes me want to run back into my room.

He grins and bends down, kissing my lips. "Let's go before Mother comes here and starts the day off on a bad note."

I'm surprised that he's brimming with excitement since he didn't seem to be too thrilled about this last night. I notice that he's dressed nicer than usual, which is a hard feat since he's always so put together. He's wearing a dressier jacket and his crown appears a little larger. He takes my hand, and we head toward the carriage.

His mother is hovering right outside the carriage. When she sees us, she's obviously disappointed that I dressed for the occasion. It clicks that this is about her showing Sam that I'm not fit to be his wife. I will give her credit for allowing him to see for himself instead of threatening and beating

Sam into submission like King Percy. Maybe she isn't as bad as I initially expected.

This carriage is even grander than the one we took from Agrolon to here. The insides look almost as if they are gold, and their trademark emerald color and jewels are everywhere. The seats are actually comfortable. Sam sits next to me, and the queen across from us.

Our hands are still entwined, and he rubs his thumb against mine. "We should be there within two hours."

We take off, and silence descends. After several minutes, the queen speaks. "So, Ariah, why did your king tell everyone you were dead?"

Straight to the point. I can't blame her for that, but it also confirms that the king told everyone I was dead. "I'm not quite sure, Your Highness."

She cuts her eyes at me. "Now, do you take me for an idiot? Why would he say that?"

Sam steps in, protecting me. "Mother, you know she was unfavored."

She turns her glare on him. "Yes, so why is she here with us?"

He gazes down at me and smiles. "Because I love her. She is the one for me."

She takes a deep breath and closes her eyes. When she opens them back up, her brown eyes find mine. "What kind of future do you really think you can have with my son? We are allies to Agrolon. We can't just keep harboring someone he tried to kill. How can you be queen? They'll want to come to your wedding, and they are dead set on Sam marrying Elizabeth. All I see is you ruining what we've tried to secure."

Sam is upset. "We will find a way. We'll elope and say she can't travel. I'm not letting her go."

Queen Lora just sighs and looks disappointed.

It seems as if the walls are closing in, and I can't breathe. I take calming breaths, reminding myself it's anxiety, but everything she said rings true. Sam is holding my hand tighter, almost as if he thinks I might slip away.

We come upon the castle, and the beauty of it stuns me. It's elegant and appears to be made of gold, similar to the carriage. Jewels are everywhere, making it stand out like a beacon. Sam smiles at my reaction. We climb out of the carriage and make our way to the main entrance. The staff is running around like crazy, welcoming their queen home.

She turns to us. "Please, give Ariah the tour. I need to go get your father. We will meet in the dining hall for lunch together before we leave to head back to the mansion."

As she walks away, my eyes take in everything. This place is shining, and I'm afraid that I might get it dirty.

The entryway is huge, with high vaulted ceilings. The insides shine with gold and emeralds glittering everywhere. There is a huge staircase with wide stairs and railings, all trimmed in gold. It's so beautiful, it almost hurts my eyes.

Sam is staring at the room as well, disgust clear on his face. "It's beautiful but a little over the top, isn't it?"

"I'm afraid I might mar something up on accident."

A corner of his lifts up and he exhales. "It's more durable than it looks, but it doesn't feel like home. That's why I like staying at the mansion."

I can understand that. It is pretty to look at, but trying to live here would be burdensome.

He takes me around the castle, showing me where he grew up and all the rooms.

Each room seems more awe-inspiring than the last, and it gets to be a little overwhelming. Pure gold is everywhere, with the emeralds embedded and shining like stars. The poor staff must really have their hands full with all that cleaning. Our last stop is the dining hall, and we find the king and queen are already sitting there waiting for us.

King Michael is clearly displeased with my presence, but he immediately turns on his diplomatic look and greets us. "Lady Ariah, please, join us for lunch." He motions for me to take a seat.

Am I really ready for this? I smile. "Thank you."

Sam pulls the chair his father had pointed to out, which happens to be across from his mother. He waits for me, and I quickly get situated. Sam pulls his own seat out and moves it closer to me so he can take my hand. The silence in the room is crippling, and no one really knows what to say. I never meant to put Sam in this position, and maybe coming with him to Orlon was a terrible mistake.

As if sensing where my thoughts are going, Sam speaks up. "I know you both aren't thrilled with my decision, but I love her. She will eventually be my bride. I gave her the family ring for when she is ready to accept my offer of marriage."

His mother cringes, but the king just nods his head, playing his part very well. "Okay, son."

It seems like forever, but the meal is over. Sam speaks up at once. "I think it's time for me and Ari to head back to the mansion. We didn't bring our things to stay overnight."

The King smiles even though it doesn't reach his eyes. "That's fine, son. Your mother and I have some things to do here, but we will see you all tomorrow. The town by the mansion has something going on that I need to attend to."

Sam leads us out and calls for a different carriage. This one that we get into is very nice, but it doesn't have as much gold, and hardly any jewels, making it obvious that we were in the king's carriage on the way here.

When the mansion comes into view, I'm so glad to be back. As soon as I can, I'm hurrying to the garden, wanting to calm my nerves. Sam stays close by and grins. "You and that garden. I'm so glad you like it."

I grin back and sit down on the grass, noticing how the greens contrast against each other. My heart sinks as I think about all the things that the queen brought up. "You know, your mother is right."

"Oh, pretty girl. Don't you worry about any of that. We will figure it out. You're mine." He bends down to kiss me, and the painful heat flares up inside.

I pull away.

He seems hurt, and that tears me apart. "I'm sorry, Sam. It's just been a long day, and a lot of things were said."

His brown eyes fill with sadness. "I know. Let's go get some dinner and just enjoy each other's company."

"That actually sounds really good." I smile, and we head to the dining hall. When we finish up, we both are exhausted, and he walks me back to my room, saying goodnight.

Changing out of the horrid dress, I quickly put my pajamas on. What if the queen is right? What repercussions will Sam face? I lay down in bed. Worry isn't going to help anything, so I push the doubts away and fall straight to sleep.

Chapter Twelve

Something is burning me, and I wake with a desperate need for coffee. Why is my necklace so hot this morning? I look at the time and realize that I've really slept in. It's only an hour before lunch, and it's strange that Sam didn't come wake me already. I quickly dress in a loose-fitting gown and ensure that my necklace is secured around my neck.

There is a knock at my door, and I open it to find Emily. I haven't seen her since the day she brought my bathing suit. "Miss, please, follow me. I think you need to be aware of something."

Okay, this is odd, but between her coming to get me and my necklace burning, something must be happening. I follow her out of my room and down the hall.

She turns to me and puts her fingers to her lips, stopping just outside a partially closed door.

Oh, it's the strategy room. What is she doing?

Soon, King Michael's voice carries down the hall. "Really,

son, you have no future with her. Please, tell me you realize this."

Oh, crap. The king and queen are already here and talking about me.

I hear pacing and Sam's tone is desperate. "We can make it work, Father. We can elope, and they never have to see her."

Something slams down, and King Michael raises his voice. "Dear goodness, boy. Are you mad? Do you think that will work? You even said she refused your proposal. Does she even know that you are engaged to Elizabeth?"

What in Knova is he talking about? How can he be engaged to her when he gave me his engagement ring? My necklace burns even hotter.

Sam's voice is angry and loud. "I didn't agree to it. You all made that arrangement. You promised me that I could marry who I wanted."

His father groans. "You should want to marry someone who is right for our Kingdom. That is your job as prince and the future king. You should want to marry into the Savior's family. Even though we won't lead, we will be right there next to them. King Percy needs us; he wants our fine things. He tries to act like they don't need it, but we know better. Do you want us to face his wrath? Do you know what he would do to us all, including her? What is going on? You've been trained for this."

There are a few moments of silence, and then Sam's tone is barely above a whisper. "I know, but I love her."

"Son, you may love her, but she's not for you. You need to cut her loose and stop stringing her along. Why would you give her that ring? That's been in my family for centuries. Elizabeth is expecting it," his father huffs.

There is a pause, but Sam finally speaks back up. "I'll get it back."

They continue to talk, but my hearing goes out. Sam, the one I expected to protect me, is about to betray me, just like Nick did. Tears pour from my eyes, and Emily takes my hand, leading me back to my room. Well, I guess it's not mine anymore.

She picks at her fingers, standing next to the door. "I'm so sorry, miss. I just wanted to let you know. The queen... Well, I've seen things and don't want you to fall victim to this family like others have."

I walk to the closet and pull out my bag, then begin filling it with clothes. "Thank you so much. I needed to know that. I have got to go now, quickly, before Sam comes for me."

"If you're leaving, let me run to the kitchen and grab you some food. I'll be right back." She runs out of the room.

Where the hell are my pants? That seamstress took them all. I don't have time to worry about it, so I just dump all the dresses in the bag that will fit. I pack everything I can, and when I'm almost finished, Emily comes back in with an alarmed Pierce.

"Here, ma'am. I have to get going. I don't want anyone to see me helping you." She heads to the door.

It takes me a second, but soon realize how much she has helped me by making sure I heard the conversation between Sam and his father. "Thank you so much. I will never forget this."

She turns, gives me a tight smile, and then leaves, shutting the door behind her.

Pierce takes in my luggage. "Ari, what's going on?"

My eyes are stinging, but I take a deep breath, trying to

level out my emotions before I cause a scene. "I have to go before Sam finds me."

Pierce nods and strolls to my back door that leads to the garden. He motions for me to follow, and we head to the stables. Luckily, Ares is there, and it seems as if he's waiting for me.

Pierce eyes widen. "You and that stallion have a strange relationship, but I'm not questioning it. We don't have time to saddle. Sam will know you've left soon enough. Can you ride bareback?"

I nod, and Ares walks over to me.

Pierce takes my bag so I can mount and then hands it back to me.

I'm about to take off when Pierce stops me. "Give me one second. I'm coming with you."

He can't do that. I don't want him to risk getting into trouble.

He disappears into the barn, cutting off my argument. Within seconds, he's coming out on a horse himself.

He's planning on coming with me. "Pierce, what are you doing? You don't need to go with me."

His golden eyes all of a sudden seem wise beyond his years. "Oh, yes, I do. You've treated me like a person. It's been a long time since someone has done that. I'm returning the favor."

Sam's shouts can be heard from the mansion. Pierce and I lock eyes and immediately leave. At this point, knowing Sam was about to betray me, I don't know what to expect from him. I'm not about to take a chance on letting someone else try to kill me.

Our horses are running into the clearing, and people are yelling back at the stables. We rush, going around the town, and hit the woods that take us in between the four kingdoms within an hour.

Ares is running fast, leading the way, and Pierce's horse is struggling to keep up. When we enter the forest, Ares slows his pace. However, he's still moving swiftly and expertly through the woods. I have no clue where he's taking us, but he seems to know where he is going.

After a while longer, Ares slows his gait to a walk. Pierce is right behind us, following our lead. "Ariah, where are you taking us?"

I turn around and shrug. "I'm not taking us anywhere. Ares is leading the way."

Pierce's jaw drops and he stares at me in disbelief. "What? You're letting that crazy stallion take us somewhere?"

"Well, yes. I have nowhere to go, so I figure he knows better than me."

Silence is my response. I turn around and see concern etched across his features. "I'm sorry, Ariah. I didn't even think."

I smile at him. "It's okay. I'll figure something out."

All of a sudden, a roar echoes around us. Ares doesn't seem fazed by it, but Pierce's horse is startled.

Pierce looks around. "What the hell is that?"

Terror wracks my body, but I'm trying to remain calm. My power springs to life and courses through me. There is a shuffling to the left of us and then a large, black bear appears between two trees. It's very angry and charges us.

Pierce hits his mare, trying to move it forward. He glances at me, pure terror in his eyes. "Run!"

Ares doesn't seem upset, as if he knows everything will be okay.

Pierce, however, is trying to go around and protect me

from the bear. His horse backs away, not wanting to go near it. The bear reaches us, and Pierce unsheathes his sword, attempting to battle it. But, even when the sword strikes it, it doesn't appear to be harming it.

How is this possible? We're going to die.

After just a few moments, the bear has overpowered Pierce, and he's slammed off the horse into a nearby tree. The bear races toward him.

Crap, if I don't do something, he's going to die. Power surges out of me and strikes the bear, bringing him to his knees. His attention is now on me and diverted from Pierce. He tries to break through but can't. The bear moans and whimpers, making me pause. In my hesitancy, the animal gets back on its paws and stares at me. Since he isn't attacking, I don't react. We stay like this for several moments until he turns and limps off, taking one last glance back at me before disappearing.

As soon as he's out of sight, I slide off Ares and head over to check on Pierce. When I reach him, his breathing is shallow, and there is a large gash on the left side of his face. If I don't get him to a healer, he's not going to make it. Selfishly, I take a moment. I'm truly alone for the first time in my entire life. No one will be here to protect me from here on out.

Swallowing, despite the lump in my throat, I bend down and hope that I can help Pierce. If I can restore the ground and earth, maybe I can heal him. I put my hands on him and close my eyes, channeling my power through him. I stay like this for a while and finally open my eyes to see that the gash has closed almost completely. Now, how am I going to get him back to Orlon?

When I stand, his horse is coming back and approaches me. Thank goodness. Lifting him with my power, I place him on the horse. He's passed out still, so I place him the best I can to make sure he won't fall off.

Looking the mare in the eye, I turn her to face the direction of home and slap her backside. I sure hope she knows what to do. I watch as she heads back, disappearing from sight. When I can't see them any longer, I drop to my knees and sob uncontrollably. I've been betrayed by Dave, Nick, and now Sam, and have no one but myself to rely on. What have I done to deserve this? Everything has been stripped away from me.

After who knows how long, Ares comes over and nudges my back. I look at him and swear understanding is in his eyes. I rise and wipe the tears and snot from my face. Okay, enough crying. I need to figure something out before night falls. This is my survival at stake. After everything, I can't fail. I won't let them win.

I mount Ares, and he takes off. In only a month's time, I had to leave my home in Agrolon, and now I don't even have Sam to rely on. I have no survival skills whatsoever, but I better get my act together and figure it out. I am going to survive just to spite everyone.

Darkness descends in the forest around me. Okay, I need to find a place to camp for the night. I at least have the obnoxious dresses to use as covers, so I should be able to find somewhere that works. Eventually, we come across a small, flat area that is wide enough for both me and the horse to rest. I pull the horrid dresses out of my bag and lay them down, making a bed. I grab some food and water and share a piece of fruit with Ares. Eventually, my eyes get heavy, and I welcome the sleep. Anything that can give me some reprieve from my broken heart.

Chapter Thirteen

The sounds of footsteps wake me from my fitful slumber. Ares is alert but doesn't look concerned. I get up, trying to gather all of my things quietly. Someone walks in front of me, and I yelp in surprise.

Owen's sister scrunches her nose up at me. "Oh, goodness. I'm surprised you made it this long. Do you really think chirping is going to scare anyone away?"

I'm not sure whether to be annoyed or relieved that Owen's sister found me. I think her name is Mer, from all the stalking I've unintentionally done. "Well, I've survived so far. Maybe it is a deterrent."

I'm so tired of people treating me like I'm disposable and worthless. The cycle stops here.

She smirks. "Maybe it's because you're just lucky."

I laugh so hard that I lose my breath.

She takes a step back, lines creasing her forehead. "Come on, let's get you to the village. We've been looking for you all night. I'm hoping things will calm down once you're there." She bends down to help gather my things.

It almost seems like she's afraid that I'm going to break down, and she's desperately trying to prevent it from happening. I reach over and grab her hands. "It's okay. I'm fine. Now, run along."

She shakes her head. "Oh, how I wish I could. However, Owen won't allow me back in without you. I don't want you to come with me, but you don't have another option. Now, get your butt up and moving. I'm hungry, and we'll be late for breakfast."

Who does she think she is? I don't even know her.

She walks over to Ares and pets him.

What? I'm the only one that he ever allows to pet him.

He nudges her like he does me, and I realize that he knows her. Is this where he was taking me this whole time? Traitor.

Fine, I'll go. Breakfast does sound good. I get up and finish packing my stuff with Mer just watching me. I guess that serves me right since I stopped her from helping a few minutes ago.

As soon as the last item is packed, Mer takes off without warning, and Ares follows right behind her.

Not wanting to get left behind, I race after them. We walk a while, but eventually, I recognize the forest I always see in my dreams. Soon, we are approaching the lake, and the sun is rising. In all my dreams, there isn't usually a lot of commotion going on in the village, but people are shouting and milling around.

When we break through the last of the trees, there are a ton of people gathering between the lake and the village. Mer shouts, "Calm down, everyone. I've found the hideaway."

The commotion stops, and as we walk up, the crowd breaks apart, letting us through. We walk straight up to

Owen, which is not surprising. His eyes focus on me, and all I want to do is reach out and touch him. Oh, hell no. I'm not doing this song and dance again.

His expression is guarded, and he looks me over. "You sure like to cause trouble, don't you?"

What a gorgeous, arrogant jerk. "Oh, yeah. That's my goal in life. I want to cause problems and be abandoned."

Mer points at me. "I told you not to mistake kindness for convenience. You brought most of this on yourself."

I pivot and scowl at her. "Don't worry. I won't make the mistake again. This has been fun, but I'm going to go now."

As I turn to leave, Owen grabs my arm. At his touch, my soul calls out to him, needing him. His condescending attitude breaks me from my stupor, thankfully. "You won't be leaving. Mer, take her to her new home. Everyone else, if you see her try to leave, bring her to me immediately."

He lets go of my arm and looks at me in disgust.

What the hell? The first time he meets me, he wants me gone and now he tells me I'm staying but looks like he hates me. I have to get away. "Hey, I thought that's what you wanted, for me to go. I don't understand why you had people searching for me, but don't worry about showing me to my new home. I'm leaving."

Owen glares at me, displeasure dripping off him. "I don't have to explain my reasoning to anyone, especially you. However, as soon as you took your first step here this morning, there was no going back. Don't try anything stupid, or you'll have to answer to me."

Mer grabs my arm, pulling me away from my face-off with Owen. I struggle against her grip, but she holds firm.

I meet her gaze. "What the hell is his problem? Owen all but pushed me out the door last time."

She takes a deep breath. "He has the full story now. If you try to leave, you won't get far and will just make things worse." She smiles cruelly. "Why don't you trust us the way you did all the other kingdoms?"

Her last statement is like a punch to my gut. She's right. I was stupid to trust all of them. It won't happen again.

We walk into one of the houses in the middle of the village, and Mer holds up both arms spinning around. "This is your new home.",

Did Owen really put me right in the middle of the village, making sure it will be as difficult as possible to sneak out? I look around and see that the inside is like all other houses where everything is made of wood. There is a small kitchen with a dining room off to the side. When I walk straight through, I wind up in the living room. There is a large couch and a side chair. There are stairs in the back corner, so I head over and walk up them.

When I step onto the second floor, there are three small bedrooms all grouped together and a bathroom on the other side. I walk into the largest room and realize it must be the main one because it has its own bathroom connected to it. It has a homey feeling, as if this is where I should have always been. I shake it off. This isn't my home, and I won't be staying here. I turn and find that Mer has followed me.

She has an expression similar to sympathy shining through her beautiful jade eyes. She walks down the stairs calling over her shoulder. "Come on, let's go eat breakfast. I'm starving."

My belly growls, and I follow her, not sure where to go. The little bit of dry meat I had for supper last night did not hold me over well.

She enters a larger house just across the street from me.

I walk in and realize it's a dining hall. This one obviously doesn't have a second floor, because it has high ceilings, about fifty tables that have been cleaned off, and a buffet in the center currently filled with eggs, bacon, and toast. At the end is a huge canister. "Please, tell me that's coffee."

Mer turns around. "Of course, it is."

Thank goodness. We walk to the buffet and each grab a plate to fill. A few seconds later, more people line up behind us and sit at an empty table, wanting to be alone. Halfway through my meal, the place is packed, and all the tables are full of people except for mine. Good, I don't need them anyway.

As I finish my meal, I'm instantly alerted that Owen has entered the room. I am very unsettled that I just know this, so I gather my trash. Before I can get up, he slides into the seat across from me.

"Hey there, princess."

Why in the world would he call me that? I'm far from a princess. "Don't call me that."

He doesn't react, just stares.

Why is he scrutinizing me? "Where did all these people come from? They all just came in at one time."

His jade eyes flash with annoyance. "Well, they were all looking for you, *princess*."

This is so strange. How did they even know to look for me? "Why were they looking for me? And my name is Ariah."

He grins cruelly and looks down at my outfit. "Well, what else are we to call you, especially in your fancy dress?"

I have to give him that. I'm in a stupid, fancy dress. "Honestly, all I have are dresses. This is what I was given at the last place I stayed. I would be more than willing to put something else on. Now, why were they looking for me?"

He's just about to answer me when a girl walks over to us.

She has long red hair and golden eyes. Her skin is tanned, from living here I assume, and she's absolutely gorgeous. Completely ignoring me, she sits close to Owen.

She rubs his arm with her hands. "Hey, I've been looking for you everywhere."

Jealousy burns deep inside me, and I want to reach over and stab her with my fork. Owen looks over at me, amusement in his eyes. He moves her hand and puts it on the table, patting her hand. "Sorry, been busy. Rose, this is Ariah, and Ariah, this is Rose."

Hearing my name from his lips has my heart pounding. Why does he have this effect on me?

Having no other choice than to acknowledge my presence, she cuts her eyes over to me and looks me up and down. "Oh, hi. So, you wear dresses? That's interesting."

I roll my eyes. She reminds me of Elizabeth. "Yeah, it looks like I do. Glad your observational skills are on par."

Owen bursts out laughing, and Rose glares with hatred clear in her eyes.

Figuring I've gotten enough enemies for the day, I get up from the table.

She smiles, glad I'm leaving, but Owen stands, too. "Speaking of clothes, let me show you where to get some different ones, if you're interested."

Rose stands and places her arm through his. "Oh, I can help her."

He detangles himself from her. "Nah, I've got this. See you later."

He leads me to the door by my arm. His touch creates so many emotions inside me, and I want to throw myself at him. This is definitely not normal. Reel it in, Ari.

When we get outside, he drops his hand. I trail behind him, trying to keep a safe distance between us. We approach another nearby house, and he walks in without knocking. As soon as I enter, due to my dream, I find myself in his home. Mer is sitting at a table by the window, sewing a pair of pants.

He leans against the door. "Got anything that will work for her?"

She pauses, unsurprised to find me. "Yeah, I do." She gets up and walks into another room. Within minutes, she comes back in with black leather pants and a black leather cropped top, which is similar in fashion to what they all wear.

He nods. "All right, I'll leave you to it." He puts his hand on the doorknob, but turns to look at me one last time before leaving. "I expect you to be at dinner. They'll come around eventually."

Him telling me what to do just burns me up. Where does he get off? However, dinner is kind of a necessity, and I don't want to push my luck. "I don't care if they come around."

He just nods his head and turns to walk out the door.

Mer tosses a shirt at me. "Get over here and try this on."

I grab the shirt and take the other clothes from her hands. I seek out a bathroom, wanting some privacy.

She waves her hand toward he door. "Don't worry, he won't be back for some time. Just change."

I just stand there a minute longer, trying to figure out an alternative. Wait. Why am I acting this way? Who cares if I have scars and what they think? So, I take a deep breath, and for the first time in my life, I strip down in front of someone, willing myself not to care, and put on the new clothes.

As I take off my dress, I feel something in it. I search for the item and realize that, somehow, Sam's emerald ring made it with me. How did that happen? I didn't put it there. Not wanting Mer to notice, I quickly finish dressing.

Mer looks me over and nods her approval. These clothes are way tighter than I'm used to, but at least they are functional.

I glance around and see a trash can in the corner. I toss the dress in.

Her forehead creases again. "Why'd you throw it away?"

"Because it serves no purpose other than to get in the way."

She looks at the trash can and back at me. "But all you own are dresses?"

I shrug, not wanting to explain myself. "Thanks for getting me some clothes. I'll see you around."

The village is bustling, which surprises me. There are people cleaning the houses and organizing food. People purposely don't look at me, which is somehow comforting, seeing how my first eighteen years was just like this. I walk through town and find myself being drawn to the lake by the cave. I take a detour to see what all this place has going on. Strolling through the outskirts, I realize that they actually grow a lot of food here, and their soil seems very healthy. Also, it looks like there is a large field just for herbs used for medicinal purposes. I eventually reach the lake and sit near the water.

Needing time to myself, I lay down on the embankment, thankful for some solitude. There is a breeze blowing off the lake and across my skin. I close my eyes and reach out to the elements, desiring to connect with them. I need some peace in my life, and my power is the only thing I now know I can rely on. When they respond, power pulses through me, bringing both comfort and relief.

Alert sounds through my head, and I quickly sit up. A noise catches my attention, and I turn to find Willow walking through the woods and over to me.

She smiles wide and sits beside me. "Hello, child. How are you?"

I chuckle at this. She doesn't look any older than forty but sounds as if she's old. "I'm fine, thanks. How are you?"

"I'm good, just anxious and ready for this to end. Your time is coming, and soon. Your faith has been tested, but now it's your time to break through. When that happens, you will find what you've always been looking for," she riddles.

I want to roll my eyes but stop myself, trying not to be visibly disrespectful. "You remind me of a few people back home. Speaking of which, where am I?"

She laughs at this, almost as if I'm not privy to an inside joke. Once again, I'm used to this, and I find it strangely comforting. "Oh, dear. No one has told you? This is Noslon."

"What? But the king is older than Owen. How is this possible?" I absorb this little bit of information and really want an answer.

Silence descends so, hopefully, Willow is going to answer my question. After a few more moments, she reaches over and touches my hand. "Why are you out here all alone?"

How do I answer this without coming off rude? I play with the ring Sam gave me, hoping she can't read my expression. "I just needed some time to breathe."

She focuses on the ring. "So, you're engaged?"

I snort, holding back tears even though they are stinging my eyes. "No, not at all. Somehow, this ring wound up here with me. He did give it to me, but he told me to wear the ring when I was ready to commit to him. However, he betrayed me. I guess I'm still trying to cling to my past."

She reaches over and squeezes my hand. "It's okay to remember but not cling. You have to focus on the future and remember the lessons you learned from the past. Until then, you cannot move forward."

For once, that makes complete sense to me, but am I strong enough to really let go? My mind flashes back to Nick, the king, and Sam, and how each betrayed me for their own selfish reasons, whether due to cowardice, greed, or self-interest.

She's right. Am I going to let those jerks keep me down, or am I going to move forward? I don't know what the future will bring, but for damn sure I'm not going to give up fighting.

I hold the ring tight in my hand, getting ready to throw it. "You're right. I think it's time to start learning how to move forward."

She holds out her hands. "Let me keep that. I think there is a purpose for it, but we will know when the time is right."

Not really caring where it ends up, I hand it over, just wanting it out of my sight.

She smiles and puts it in her pocket.

I rise from the ground, realizing she won't leave anytime soon, and glance down. "I'm going to head out. Thanks for the talk."

Wanting to get some distance from all the puzzles, I make my way back to the house. I head straight to the bathroom and take a nice long shower. Something I learn quickly is trying to put back on tight, leather clothing when you're soaking wet is very difficult. I need to find some pajamas to sleep in.

Stomping toward Owen's place, I knock on the door. Mer opens it and gives me a strange look.

I point to my outfit. "I need another pair of clothes and pajamas."

She smirks. "Are you sure? You left here completely content with the clothes you have on."

I cross my arms. "I needed some space, but I realized that I might need a few things."

She tilts her head, amused. I'm not willing to deal with her, so I turn around. "Just forget it. I'll figure something out."

I head back to my place and pull the dreadful dresses out. I turn on the tub and wash the clothes, since they'd been on the forest floor. I hang them up to dry and go in search of scissors and thread. Using my power, I pull the water out of the clothes, so they are immediately dry. Why the heck didn't I think to do that when I got out of the shower?

I cut up the dresses and hem them into pajamas. They look like a kindergartener sewed them, but at least I didn't have to beg for something. It'll work. Who's going to see me in my pajamas anyway?

Content with my hard work, the loud knock at the door startles me out of my trance. I open the door up to find a man standing there. He has blonde hair, hazel eyes, and looks like a freaking warrior. He is gorgeous, but there is a hardness to him.

He glances inside the house. "Hey, I'm Jacob. Owen asked me to come get you for dinner. Let's go."

Dinner sounds good, so I'm not going to argue. I tag behind him and walk into the dining area that is brimming with people. I go through the buffet line and grab my food. Not wanting to try to find a place to sit, I'm about to head out when someone steps in front of me.

"Hey there, gorgeous. You can join me," someone states. I

look up to find an average-looking guy standing there. He isn't attractive, but he isn't ugly. He has shaggy, mousy brown hair with brown eyes that almost match. He is a little thick but has a very jovial smile. I can't help but smile back at him.

Taking my response as an invitation, he takes my plate from me and leads me to a table. Before I can get there, Owen jumps up from his spot.

He snatches my plate from Smiley, then turns to me. "You'll be joining me for dinner. We have things to discuss."

Tired of being told what to do, I snatch my plate from him. "No, I'm good. I already told Smiley here that I'd sit with him. We can talk later."

The dining hall goes quiet, and I force myself not to shrink back and blend in. That hasn't served me well before, so I'm going to try something new. I sit down at the table the nice guy was leading me to, and someone plops down beside me.

"You all can find a different table to eat at," Owen commands from beside me.

Everyone gets up from the table as fast as possible. A few seconds later, Jacob sets his food down, joining us. Great, mister moody and warrior are the last two people I want to spend time with. Of course, they would be friends.

Owen looks down and sighs. "So, you're already getting hit on?"

Jacob snorts, and I'm bewildered. "This is what we had to discuss?"

He sits back and clears his throat. "No, I was just curious. You haven't even been here a day."

I huff and continue eating.

Jacob shakes his head and takes a drink of his water.

Silence descends, and I welcome it. After a few moments, I feel Owen tense up beside me.

Cringing, a voice that makes me want to vomit rings in my ear. "Oh, there you are, baby. I've been looking all over for you." Rose saunters over to us and sits down on the other side of Owen.

Jealousy surfaces, but I immediately attempt to quash it. Men are bad news, especially that one. He scoots closer to me, making our arms touch, and yearning immediately overtakes me. He looks at me, and I'm lost in a trance.

Rose clears her throat, not wanting to be ignored. The sound is enough to break the spell, and I put some distance between us. I find something I don't recognize in Owen's eyes, but he shuts down whatever was churning.

He groans. "Rose, please, stop calling me baby, and I've been busy."

She reaches out to stroke his arm, and for some reason, I'm about ready to come unglued. Before she can touch him, he captures her hand, placing it on the table.

I finish up and rise from my seat.

He looks up confused. "Where are you going?"

I turn, surprised at his attention. "To the house. I'm done eating. Where else am I supposed to go?"

Rose flips her hair. "Oh, yeah, are you going to be a free-loader your entire time here?"

This comment pushes me over the edge, and anger overcomes me. "No, I don't plan on it at all. However, I wasn't sure where to help. Let me know what tasks are available and I'll gladly start."

She opens her mouth to speak, but Owen cuts her off. "We need you to start training with your power, but wanted to give you time to assimilate here."

Rose's mouth drops open and she narrows her eyes. "Wait, no one trains unless it's on weaponry. We've been told practicing our power will lower our barrier. Why am I not training?"

His face turns rigid and his tone harsh. "Because we don't need you to. You need to focus on learning medicine."

"But I have some of the darkest hair here, besides your sister and the new visitor with the strange red hair that looks to be turning black. I bet she doesn't have any power... Oh, I see," she smirks.

Owen ignores her and looks at me. "Meet me here so we can have breakfast, then I'll show you where to train."

I salute. "Aye, aye, sir." And head to the door. As soon as I'm outside, I am more at ease. The moon is shining, and I'm away from the crowd.

When I get home, I get ready for bed, and as soon as I hit the sheets, I'm out.

Chapter Fourteen

✦❧✦

I braid my dark hair so that it falls down my back and realize that the red is almost gone. Wonder if any of those berries are around here? I quickly brush my teeth and rush to the banquet hall. I find that Jacob and Owen are already there eating breakfast, so I make my plate and head to a vacant table. When I'm about halfway done, Owen makes his way over to me.

He slides into the seat across from me. "So, you finally decided to get up?"

"Yeah, I figured it was about time."

I take the last few bites of my food and quickly stand up.

He rises, too, and frowns. "You didn't have to rush."

I shrug and clean up my mess. "No, it's okay. I'm actually really ready to train."

He nods, and I follow him out the door.

We walk past the lake and away from the village. I'm wondering where he is taking me, and soon, another clear patch opens up in the forest.

There is Willow, sitting on the ground, waiting for us. She

purses her lips. "Well, hello. It's about time you both got here."

I'm about to speak up, but Owen beats me to the punch. "Sorry. I was up late with an issue and then just had a slow beginning. It won't happen again."

She nods, but her attention is on me. "So, a little birdie told me you had some powers. I would love to see what you can do."

I'm about to deny it but figure, if this is what they need me to do to earn my keep, well, I'll suck it up. I nod, and she grins.

She walks over to gather a larger stick and lays it down a few feet in front of me. "Now, I want to see you pick only that stick up."

Owen scoffs, but I just ignore him. I'll prove him wrong. I connect to my power and ask it to help with the branch. The churning starts, and soon, I have the branch up in the air with nothing else blowing in the air around it.

Owen gasps.

Willow grins, her eyes filled with excitement. "Excellent. It's time to really begin."

⚓

I haven't been this worn out since training with Lydia. Willow pushed to see how much I could do after she made Owen leave. I'm so glad she did, because he's just a distraction — one I can't afford to have around.

After making tornados and fireballs, I'm dragging to the cottage. I heard Willow muttering about what tomorrow will bring, but I'm too tired to listen. When I approach my destination, I'm startled to find Owen standing by the door. He glances up at my approach, and concern etches his face. "Are you okay?"

Not having the energy to nod my head, I softly answer. "Yes."

He hurries and opens the door for me, and I stumble onto the couch, lying down. "Ariah, I'm going to go get you something to eat. Have you been training this entire time?"

I grab a pillow and close my eyes. "Yeah, I know. My endurance will improve."

He pauses, his eyes widening. "You've been gone for over ten hours and missed lunch. M... Willow didn't give you a break?"

Ten hours? I slowly raise my body back up to look out the window and realize that it is dusk. I didn't even notice that on the way in. I plop back down on the couch, not having the strength to say upright. "No, but honestly, I didn't realize it had been so long."

The door shuts, I realize I'm alone, just like I will always be from here on out. For once, instead of getting sad, I get angry. How dare the two most important men in my life betray me like that? How I miss Logan, Claire, and my Mother. I continue down my dark thoughts, almost on the cusp of sleep, when someone enters the house.

I try to get up, but I can't. My body is plastered to the couch. Much to my relief, it's Owen that comes into view. He has a plate full of food and a drink. He sets the items on the table and bends to help me sit up. He moves pillows around me so that I am more comfortable. Who is this nice person? Did he fall and hit his head?

He hands me my food and drink. "I put some herbs in your drink that should help you bounce back. I'm sorry she was so rough on you."

"Honestly, I enjoyed every minute. My power is always brimming, and I always seem to be struggling to maintain control. For once, it's not pulsing to come out, and I enjoyed the training," I take a huge sip of the beverage. I figure, at this point, if he was trying to kill me, I'd already be dead.

He stays silent for a while, and I eat, suddenly ravenous. I quickly devour the food and quench my thirst. Then I catch him watching me. Oh, no. Did he just watch me eat like I haven't seen food in ages?

He leans over to get my empty plates, and his arm brushes mine. We lock eyes, and I can't make myself look away. He slowly leans down and places his lips on mine.

It is a brief kiss, but it steals my breath. The sensation is overwhelming. Before now, I've never truly been kissed before. My lips tingle, and I'm instantly rejuvenated. The cup falls to the floor, breaking the connection.

He bends to pick it up and places it on the table. He then runs his hands through his hair, shock clear on his face. "It can't be true." He stands up, panic clear on his face. "I hope you get to feeling better. I have to get going. See you around."

He walks out the door without a backward glance, leaving me with a huge mess. Well he's back to his normal, curt ways. I slowly get up from the couch, putting my empty dishes on the table. I'll clean up in the morning. Right now, I want to go to bed.

Chapter Fifteen

The next few weeks are similar. Owen avoids me at all costs and seems to have taken an interest in the horrid Rose. I train with Willow every day and just try to keep out of the way.

I make my way over to the dining hall to get breakfast. Over the past few weeks, my powers have grown, and I'm learning how to use them effectively. I walk into the room and head to the buffet to make my plate. I don't bother looking around. One, I still do not want to get to know anyone, and two, I do not want to see Rose fawning all over Owen. He's a jerk, so it shouldn't matter, but for some reason, it does.

I make my way to my standard table and dig in. A few moments later, Mer sits next to me. "Hey, Ariah. When you get done here, let's go to my house."

Looking up, is she really here and sitting next to me? I haven't talked to her in weeks, and for some reason, she's being nice again. She must want something. Not wanting to ruin my meal with drama, I nod.

She smiles and giggles. She is beautiful, and even though she always wears black, she has a multitude of outfits. She rises from her seat. "I'll be waiting for you."

I nod and focus on my task, which is getting this French toast in my belly. After finishing, I head over to her house, hoping and praying that Owen isn't there. I knock on the door and startle when he opens it up.

He looks concerned. "Ariah, are you okay?"

What a jerk. How dare he act like he cares. The last time I saw him, he gave me the best kiss I've ever had, but he has avoided me since and ran to Rose. Nope, not happening.

"I'm here for Mer."

His eyebrows shoot up. "Mer? She lets you call her that? Why are you looking for her, and why here? Is everything alright?"

He steps toward me, and I move backward. Getting close to him is not good for my brain or my heart. "Yeah, she said to come to her house when I'm done." I wave my arm in front of my body. "So, here I am."

He bites his lip, his face clearly amused. "You think she lives here? Have you not talked to anyone?"

I look past him into the house. "Well, the last time I saw her, it was here."

His smile breaks through. "Yeah, because she was here fixing some of my clothes. Come on, I'll take you to her."

Once again, I'm following behind him but make sure I keep a safe distance back. We walk past a few houses when he stops.

He glances back with a puzzled expression and eventually knocks on her door.

So what if I'm ten feet behind? I'm not chancing another accidental touch. I learned after my first mistake.

Mer answers the door and seems put off when she realizes it's Owen. "What do you want? I'm expecting someone."

He points to me. "You mean her?" He grins at Mer. "She thought we lived together."

Mer laughs. "Oh, you'd be dead by now."

I speak without thought. "Just be glad you have one another. My brother thinks I'm dead."

They both to look at me with an expression I can't read.

Yep, I still have excellent social skills. Why did I just volunteer that information?

Mer snaps out of it first and turns to Owen. "Tell Willow that Ariah will be a few minutes late. I need to talk to her."

"Oh, I can stay," he offers.

She holds up her hand, telling him to stop. "Nope, you go. Ariah and I need some alone time."

Owen stares at her for a moment, almost as if he's searching for answers. When he is satisfied, he moves past me and waves goodbye.

I stay where I am until he's out of sight.

She steps out of the doorway and waves me in. "Come on in."

I walk into her home, and once again, it's just like all the others, but it has a unique touch with all of her sewing supplies and material out.

She takes in my outfit and grins. "So, you really like that outfit I gave you, huh?"

I don't react, seeing as it's the only thing I have to wear other than the pajamas I made out of those awful dresses.

She laughs. "Despite my best efforts, I've grown to like you. You aren't anything like I expected, and you aren't trying to weasel your way into our home. So, I figure I should give you some things that might make your life easier."

She stands by a pile of clothes and picks them up. There are at least five different outfits for me and some comfortable-looking pajamas. She hands them to me, but I don't take them.

I look at the clothes and back at her. "What do you want?"

She takes a step back, and her eyebrows lift. "What do you mean?"

"The first time I saw you, I thought you were nice, but you were quick to correct me. I believe you said something to the extent of 'don't mistake kindness for convenience', and I realized you're right. So, what do you want?"

For whatever reason, her smile grows, but there is sadness reflecting in her eyes. "So, you're not so gullible anymore, huh? It's true what I said, but this is neither kindness nor convenience. I know you've been working hard and not asking for anything in return. You've earned this so, please, take it."

I take the clothes against my better judgment, but I'm so tired of scratchy night clothes and washing my one outfit every night. "Fine, as long as I've earned it."

She grins at me, and I turn to head out. "Hey, Ariah. Do you mind if we sit together at dinner tonight? I really need to get a break from Rose's slobber, Owen's moodiness, and Jacob's cold shoulder."

I glance back and shrug. "Yeah, sure, I guess." I continue on my way back to my home to drop off my clothes.

When I get to the field, I find Willow there talking with Owen. Great, after not seeing him much for a month, I run into him twice before lunch. Willow doesn't look very happy about him being here, but he seems to be holding his ground.

"Hey, are we not training today?"

She turns to me and rolls her eyes. "Yes, we are, but Owen wants to watch."

I cross my arms and shake my head. "Nope. Not going to happen. If he stays, I go."

Willow smirks, and Owen leans back against a tree. His forehead creases. "Who do you think you are?"

"I think I'm someone who isn't comfortable around you. You're nice one minute then an ass the next. You mess with my head, and I don't want you here while I'm trying to concentrate." I put my hands on my hips. "Either you leave, or I will."

"I'll leave when I want to," he retorts, marching toward me.

I turn and head back toward the village.

"Owen." Willow's tone holds a warning. "Just leave her alone."

A glance back shows her standing between us, but Owen steps around her and reaches for my hand, pulling me back around.

The buzzing springs to life, and I drop his hand.

His eyes are slits at this point. "Where do you think you're going?"

I cross my arms and take a step back, needing distance. "Back home. I'm not training with you."

Willow bursts out laughing. "She's not like all the other girls. I warned you."

Owen scowls and focuses back on me. "If I want to be here, I have every right."

I will not back down. I'm tired of being pushed around. If he doesn't like it, I can leave. "And if I don't want to be here, I have every right."

He takes a menacing step toward me. "This is how you earn your keep around here. You don't have much choice."

Oh, no, he didn't. I turn and walk fast back to my house, with him yelling my name in the background. I refuse to be treated like this *ever* again. For some reason, my heart is ripping in two, and I ridiculously want to go talk to him and make things 'right'. But I refuse to be that weak again. The cycle stops here.

I slam the door and flop on the couch. My heart is breaking for everything I've lost, and flashes of my past flitter through my mind. I let the hurt in and welcome the pain for the very first time, and somehow, it's a relief. Sure, I've cried, but for the first time ever, I mourn all the things that I have lost. First and foremost, I ache for my brother, Claire, my mother, and lastly, for my innocence and trust. Nick, my childhood friend, totally betrayed me, and now Sam has as well.

No one is as they seem, and I'll be damned if I make that mistake again. After wallowing for a while, I realize it's dinner time. I get up, wash my face, and head to the dining hall. As soon as I walk through the door, my eyes zero in on Rose hanging all over Owen.

He doesn't seem to mind it until he sees I've walked into the room. He glances up at me.

I ignore him as I try to hold it together. I make my food and sit down in my usual seat.

Mer slams her food down on the table, taking a seat across from me. "Thank goodness, you're here. I can't stand being around him and Rose. She's so pathetic."

I force an expression of indifference. I don't want her to see how much them being together affects me.

She stuffs a forkful of food in her mouth, and I take a

deep breath and join her. After a short while, Owen walks over and sits beside me.

Mer points at him. "Owen, go back over there before Rose comes over. I can't watch anymore."

He stiffens beside me, but I ignore him. It's one of the hardest things I've ever done.

Within seconds, Rose makes her presence known. She sits down beside him, rubbing her hand up and down his arm. "Oooooowwweennn, why did you leave me over there all alone with Jacob? You know he scares me."

I can't take it any longer. I'm at my limit. I get up, startling everyone, and turn to leave.

Owen's jaw stiffens. "Ariah, where are you going?"

I just need to get out of here and away from him. Why is he stopping me? I turn. "Why does it matter to you? Just focus on Rose and her needs."

Owen jerks back like he's been slapped.

Rose looks like the cat that ate the canary.

I march out of the dining hall and head straight to the house. My emotions are running high, and I can't stay here any longer. For some reason, my soul is totally invested in Owen, and distance is needed.

I grab the few things that I have in the house and make sure the necklace is still secured around my neck. Luckily, I have a little food in the pantry, so I put some jerky and canned food into my bag. I go out the back door of the house, so not everyone will see me if they are looking through the windows of the dining hall.

Within minutes, I'm passing the river and breaking into the woods. I walk a little way, the moon lighting the sky, and there is movement coming from the left. My power rages, and then Ares comes out through the trees and into the light.

JEN L. GREY

My heart resumes a normal pace, my erratic breathing calms, and a smile fills my face.

"Hey, boy. I haven't seen you in a while. Where have you been?"

He walks over to me and I pet his forehead. He huffs and I chuckle. I jump on his back, and he heads back toward the Noslon village. "No, Ares. We are going somewhere else. I don't want to go back there," I call out.

He huffs but turns, much to my relief. We move through the woods for a while, and honestly, I'm not sure where to go. Soon, Ares stops moving, and I realize he found a good spot for us to rest for the remainder of the night. I jump off him and pull out the covers I had stripped from the bed. I lay them on the ground underneath some trees and then gather some limbs to start a fire.

When everything is settled, I crawl on top of the sheets, trying not to overthink my situation. I have no plan, but there is always tomorrow morning to figure it all out. I close my eyes and fall into a deep slumber.

Chapter Sixteen

Someone is calling my name. "Ariah. Ariah."

I startle awake at the sound. How in Knova have they already found me? I get up as quietly as I can and start packing. I can hear shuffling in the woods and know someone is getting closer. I turn to find Ares near me, and I jump on his back.

He isn't thrilled about leaving, but he appeases me by moving in the opposite direction.

We walk a little further before Mer walks out in front of us. "Hey there, runaway. Where are you heading?"

What the hell? This is the second time she's found me. "How do you keep finding me?"

She laughs and just shakes her head. "Come on. You've made your point, and it's time to go home."

"I don't have a home."

She huffs and rolls her eyes. "Yes, you do. You'll realize it in time."

Is she really trying to speak in riddles now, too? "Oh, are you channeling Willow?"

She grins and wiggles her eyebrows. "Like mother like daughter, right?"

Wow. Did she just admit that she is their mother? "Owen always calls her Willow."

She rolls her eyes. "That's because he's our king. He's weird. He thinks he should call her by her first name."

She moves in the direction of the village, expecting me to follow, but I stand still. She lets out a breath and turns to me. "Come on. Things will be better now."

"What? Why do you think something is wrong?"

She barks out a laugh. "Oh, come on. I know things. It'll be better. Let's go before Owen completely loses it."

I really want to stand my ground, but honestly, I don't have anywhere else to go. Can I really afford to let my pride get in the way of survival? I'm sure Owen is losing it because he's afraid I'll tell everyone about their precious hidden little village. No wonder no one has heard from Noslon in years.

Swallowing my ego, I follow behind her. She smiles, but it's not out of malice. Why is she being so nice to me? Ever since the beginning, she's been standoffish and blunt, so why the change?

Ares follows behind us, and Mer looks back at the stallion and points her finger at him. "Why am I not surprised you are here, troublemaker?"

He hangs his head, almost like he understands her.

When did crazy become the norm in my life?

Ares butts his head against my back, nudging me forward.

Mer smirks. "Trying to redeem yourself?"

Ares stomps and nudges me again.

We make our way back toward the village. We arrive back at lunch since I honestly didn't get very far from the grounds.

I'm surprised to find that no one is out working, tending to their daily chores. Where is everyone?

We walk up toward my cottage, and I find everyone out in the square right in front of the dining hall.

Owen is standing in the middle, and as soon as I come into view, his eyes immediately land on me.

Jacob and Willow are standing next to him.

Owen keeps his eyes on me, heading in our direction. "Jacob, call the search off. Our little runaway has been found."

Jacob nods his understanding.

Owen's rage is clear on his face.

To my surprise, Mer steps in front of me, blocking him from me.

Owen growls. "Get out of the way, Mer."

She places her hands on her hips, standing her ground. "No, not happening. You need to cool off."

Oh, no. I appreciate what Mer is trying to do, but I've learned that you can't count on anyone but yourself. I step around her.

And she glares at me.

Owen gives me a sinister smile. "Oh, look, the little butterfly is trying to sprout its wings."

I put my hands on my hips. How dare he still look gorgeous? "Back off. I don't have time for your mind games."

"Like hell, I will. How dare you run away. What if something happened to you?"

"Then," I point to him, "I guess you'd be down one less problem."

His face turns blood red. "You are right. I'd certainly have one less problem."

Mer goes to stand between us yet again, but Willow stops her. I didn't even realize she had moved to where we are.

I wave my hand toward Mer. "Then, why did you send her to find me? Just let me stay out there."

"There is no way that's happening." He crosses his arms, daring me to challenge him. "This is your home, and you're staying."

My power pulses out of me, slamming into him. I pin him to the ground, but unexpectedly, there is a resistance to my power. Having never experienced it before, I have no clue what's going on until Owen gets to his feet and bounces my power off him like he has a shield. The only people capable of that are power wielders like me.

He gets in my face. "Don't use your power on me unless you're ready for a battle."

He grabs my arm and drags me into his house. Before I can react, his mouth is on mine, but this kiss is different than the last one we shared. This is urgent and needy and completely undoes me. Finally, a little sense filters back into my brain, and I pull away.

He is breathing raggedly, and his eyes are glazed. "What's wrong?"

Tears are stinging my eyes, but I hold them back. "I can't do this."

I turn to leave, but he shoves me against his wall, trapping me between his arms. "You're not leaving, Ariah. I need you right now. You leaving last night made me crazy."

I snort and reply, "You seemed to be doing fine with Rose."

I move to go under his arm, but he grabs my hands, pinning them above my head. "She means nothing to me. It's over."

"Oh, and you think that I'll just let you run straight to me? No way that's happening. I won't be fooled a third time."

He grins, which catches me off guard. "You think you actually have a choice?"

Damn, why does he have to be so hot? The pleasant buzzing under my skin is not helping. "Yep, sure do, and you're not it."

He shakes his head. "Believe me, you wouldn't be my choice either."

I knee him in the crotch, catching both of us off guard. He falls to the ground in pain, and I take off out of the house. That's what he gets for trying to be overbearing.

Rushing into my house, I slam the door and bolt it. There is something weird going on between us, and obviously, there is more to him than what meets the eye. I try to push him from my mind, seeing that Mer dropped my bag off here while I was preoccupied. Thankful, I grab an outfit out of the bag and jump in the shower, washing the filth off me.

After getting ready and feeling human, I leave and take a walk, trying to cool off. When I'm walking past one of the medicinal fields, someone shouts out. I'm surprised to find Smiley heading my way.

He winks at me. "Hey there. You sure like to make a fuss, don't you?"

I smile back, confused. "What do you mean?"

When he approaches, I notice dark circles under his eyes. He rubs his rubs. "We all were out looking for you all night. Owen was about to flip his lid."

"Oh, well, he's ornery like that. The only time he smiles is when he's being a jerk or telling people what to do."

Smiley cracks up and nods his head. "That's true, but I've

never seen him that worked up over anything before. Rose seemed very displeased. Are you and him a thing?"

"Oh, gosh no. We can barely tolerate each other. I don't know why he was acting that way." I put my fingers to my lips. "Maybe he doesn't want to lose the power wielder he's been having trained."

He glances down and picks at his fingernails. "Well, good. Since you guys aren't an item, I was hoping you might want to come to my place for dinner."

I almost say no, but having dinner with him means I won't have to go to the dining hall and face Owen. And, really, Smiley is nice and pleasant to be around. "Yes, I'd like that."

His head jerks up, and somehow, his smile gets even bigger. "Yeah?"

I giggle at his reaction. "Yes, I'd love to."

"Okay, I'll pick you up at five. Oh, and by the way, my name is Steve."

I grin. "Okay, Steve. I'll be ready at five. Oh, I live..."

He holds his hands up, cutting me off. "I know where you live. I'll see you then." He turns to walk away.

Happy with the plans, I continue my walk, lost in thought. I think Steve and I could be friends. He seems genuine and easy to be around.

Ugh, I need to get home, so I can clean up before dinner. I hurry to the cottage and unpack my bag so when I get home tonight, I can go straight to bed. Sleeping on the forest floor is not conducive for a good rest. A few minutes before five, there is a knock at my door.

I open it without thought and find Owen standing there.

He gauges my reaction, and a scowl comes across his face. "Were you expecting someone else?"

I tilt my head. Why does he keep bothering me? "Uh, yes, I was. What do you want?"

He takes a step closer to me. "Who did you think it was?"

"Just someone else. Does it matter?"

He looks around. "Yes, it matters. Did you think it was my sister?"

"No, I didn't." I walk outside, shutting the door behind me. "Once again, why are you here?"

"I came here to get you for dinner."

I open my mouth, but someone clears their throat, cutting me off.

Owen turns around and glowers at Steve. "What are you doing here?"

Steve taps his foot, fidgeting. "Oh, um… Ariah and I have dinner plans."

Owen steps toward him. "No, you don't."

"Uh… hello. I'm right here, and yes, we do." I step in front of Owen and smile up at Steve.

Owen ignores me, pulling me behind him and taking another menacing step toward Steve. "She has plans with me. Sorry, don't ask her again."

White hot anger stirs in me again. "No, I don't have plans with you. Steve and I already had a mutual agreement tonight. Maybe you should try asking sometime. Being a little nicer might work better on people."

"Oh, princess, you see, I don't have to be nice. I'm in charge here, and people do what I say. Now that you're here, the same rules apply to you. It's cute that you think other-wise," he growls.

I get in his face, refusing to back down. "You see, I've been pushed around my entire life, and I'm tired of it. Maybe you should stop looking for me, since I will not obey you."

Steve is very uneasy, and I hate that he's put into this situation. I move around Owen and grab his hand. "Have a nice night. Tell Rose I said hi."

Owen looks bewildered, his jade eyes wide. "Ariah, get your ass back here this instant."

But I continue on, pulling Steve right with me.

Mer shouts, "Leave her alone. Stop being a prick. Maybe if you were nicer, she wouldn't keep running off."

For some reason, she's been helping me more and more. I don't even want to try to analyze that one right now.

Steve breaks the silence once we are a safe distance away. "Uh, Ariah. Is this a good idea? I don't want Owen pissed at me. He can kind of make my life a living hell."

Ugh, I didn't think about that, but the damage is already done. "I'm sorry. I just can't take being controlled anymore. I didn't think of the repercussions for you, though."

His smile lights up his face once again. "Oh, that's fine. I can handle it. I just worry about you."

"Don't worry about me. I've been hurt and am still going." I meant to say it kiddingly, but it falls flat.

We are silent for a few minutes, and I regret saying what I have. At least, my social skills haven't changed. That should be comforting, right? We continue walking.

Steve reaches up and scratches his ear. "Uh, mind if I lead the way now? We are getting further and further from my house."

Oh, my goodness. In my anger, I just took off, needing to get away. He must think I'm crazy. "Oh, I just had to get out of there. I didn't even think about that."

He grins, and it makes him more handsome. He's not attractive like Owen at all, but his smile makes it seem like everything is going to be all right. In a way, it reminds me of

Claire. Of course, thinking of her causes pain, but I never want to forget my beautiful, happy, loyal first friend.

His cottage is more on the outskirts, close to the medicinal field. When we walk in, I take in the room. His interior is similar to mine but slightly older. He has a kitchen, but his appliances look a little more dated, and there are drying herbs and bottles of medicine littering his countertop.

He cringes. "Sorry, we kind of use our homes to make our medicines. We do have a local healing station that we stock, but our supplies are so ample that we keep what we make in our houses."

I walk over to a bottle that contains a green, pasty substance. "Oh, no worries. It's very intriguing. We didn't have medicines like this at home. What are these?"

"Those are antibiotic ointments. They are actually stronger than the oral kind, but the infection has to be on the skin. If the ointment can't touch the injury, then it won't work."

He grins at me and walks over to the oven, pulling out the food. It smells delicious.

I walk over to see what it is. It's soup and has meat and colorful vegetables in it.

He waves his hand over the food. "This, my friend, is venison and vegetables. One of my friends went hunting the other day and caught a large buck. This is a family recipe, and I guarantee you'll love it."

My stomach grumbles. "Okay, I'm starving. Load me up."

When I taste the soup, I'm surprised that he's right. This is the best meal I've had in a long time. I devour my first bowl and find him watching me.

He smirks. "Want another bowl?"

I pout. "Yes, please. I'm not above begging."

"Oh, begging is not necessary," he winks.

It's so easy being around him. He's very open about himself and quick to answer my questions. I learn that his family has passed away, and he loves working in the fields and making medicine.

"It's my way to contribute to our village and help everyone. I make a cream that helps older people with their aches and pains, medicines to help people who are sick, and even some that help infants who have a hard time feeding," he explains passionately.

I need to find a cause like that. "That's a good cause, and I hope one day I can find a way to help people like you're doing."

He reaches out and squeezes my hand. "Oh, Ariah. You'll be helping them more than me. Don't you know the war is near? Why do you think Owen has you training like you are?"

I glance up, surprised at his words. "What do you mean?"

"We haven't had a female strong enough to train in decades. It's one reason why he doesn't want to lose you. The West is rallying, and the North and South won't take it. The war is coming, and the Savior is in place. It won't be long before she turns eighteen." He glances at my hair, removing his hand. "Although, it is strange that you have black hair."

It's funny how everyone in Agrolon and Orlon thought I was weak and worthless, and now, here, Owen thinks I'm powerful enough to train, even with my dark hair. My eyes start sagging, and I realize I need to get home. I stand up, and Steve glances outside. "Come on, I'll walk you home. I'm sure you didn't sleep well last night." I smack him on the arm, and he laughs.

When we walk up to my house, there is someone

standing by my door. It's Owen, and I really don't want to face him, even if my body wants to run to him.

Steve laughs and stops. "I think it's best if you finish the way by yourself. I don't want to be beat up tonight."

I understand him not wanting to go any further. "Oh, great. Throw me to the wolves."

He pats me on my shoulder. "If I didn't think you could handle it, I wouldn't leave. However, I have a feeling you'll do just fine."

He turns to head back home, and I say, "Traitor," causing him to laugh even more. I take a deep breath and continue my march to my door.

Owen is leaning against my door with his arms crossed against his chest. His muscles are defined in his shirt making him look even better than normal, and I make my eyes look back up at his face. His jade eyes are staring down at me. "Have a good night?"

I stop a few feet away from him. "Actually, I did. It's amazing how nice it is when the person you are with is pleasant."

He sighs and runs his hands through his hair. "Can we talk?"

I put my hand on my chest. "Wow, I'm being asked?"

He groans. "Please?"

Okay, he's never been this nice to me before, so against my better judgment, I open my door and hold it open for him.

He seems surprised by my gesture, but walks in, almost like he's afraid I'll change my mind.

I shut the door, but stay right in front of it. "What do you need?"

"I want to ask for a do-over."

Wasn't expecting that. "A do-over?"

"Yes, I've been out of line and a little crazy." He's tapping his foot and biting his top lip.

I lean back against the door, enjoying his awkward demeanor. "And overbearing, and a jerk?"

"Let's not push it," he grumbles. "I'm... sorry."

Never in a million years did I expect to hear those words come out of his mouth. "It's okay."

"No, it's not. Look, we didn't start on the right foot, but..." he pauses.

My heart picks up its pace. What is he getting at? "But..." I encourage.

He looks up at the ceiling. "I'd like to get to know you better."

"Wow. That sounds sincere."

He moans at my statement and runs a hand down his face. "Ugh... Why are you making this so hard? I want to court you, okay?"

My heart is full-on galloping now. Before I realize what I'm doing, I've already answered. "Okay."

He visibly relaxes at the comment and hesitantly steps toward me. "Are you sure?"

What am I doing? Could I bear it if his changed his mind? "Yes, but are you? I thought you didn't want me around."

He takes a hesitant step toward me, his face full of remorse. "I didn't mean it like it sounded. I'm not upset with you but, rather, the situation. Look, I'll tell you more when the time is right. Just, right now, I'd like to get to know you without all the fighting."

I have to set boundaries and make sure he's serious. I can't take my heart being trampled on again. "Okay, but if you're a jerk, I'm out. If you are going to play games with Rose, I'm out. I'm not going to be mistreated or used."

He nods. "I totally respect that. No more dinners with Steve or anyone else. If we are doing this, it's exclusive for both of us."

Butterflies take flight in my belly, but the cynic in me still sounds warning bells in my head. "Fine, exclusive, but we take it slow."

He smirks and gives me a wink. "I'll go as fast as you want."

I cross my arms. I refuse to be lured in by his cocky ways. "All right, but I need to go to bed. I'm exhausted."

He smirks. "That's what you get for running away."

I stick my tongue out at him, and for the first time ever, he truly laughs. It's breathtaking, and I want to kiss him.

He must be able to read my signals, because he moves toward me, trapping me in between his arms with the wall to my back. He lowers his lips to mine, and our kiss is sweet and intense. I lose track of time, but he eventually pulls away.

My body is on fire, and my lips tingle from his.

"Goodnight, princess. I'll pick you up for breakfast." He brushes his lips against mine once more and walks out my door.

I lock it and head straight to bed.

Chapter Seventeen

⁂

The sunlight streams through my window, causing me to wake. I squint in the light and get out of bed. Oh, crap. Owen will be here soon, and I'm not dressed. I pull my hair back into a braid, pouting when I realize the red is all gone from my hair. After getting dressed, I sit down in the living room and wait.

After a while, I get up, annoyed that I'm already reverting back to my old ways. Why am I just hovering, hoping he'll come? I know where to get breakfast. Pissed at myself for being so pathetic, I head into the dining hall and get in line for the buffet. Thoughts of him try to invade my mind, but I don't allow it. I will not go back to being that same girl, always depending on others.

When I finish loading my plate up, I look around and find that Steve is at a vacant table. I make my way to him and sit down across from him.

He stares at my plate and then glances up. "Hungry much?"

So what if my plate is loaded with food to the point that

some of its falling off the sides? I never proclaimed not to be an emotional eater. "Yup, sure am."

He chuckles. "So, what happened last night? You know, after I left."

This is the last thing I want to talk about, seeing as I'm supposed to be keeping him from my mind, but I don't want to be rude. Steve's a nice guy. "Made a stupid decision and regret it this morning."

He's about to push for more when Owen walks into the room, and obviously, Steve notices him as well.

Only a few seconds later, Owen is sitting right next to me. "I thought I said I'd pick you up for breakfast."

I shrug my shoulders, focusing on stuffing my face. "Yeah, well, I got hungry."

He turns and glares at Steve. "It's funny that I find him with you last night and again first thing in the morning."

Steve clears his throat and avoids eye contact.

I slam my fork down on the table. "Look, quit acting like a jerk. Yeah, you said that you would pick me up for breakfast, but I'm not going to sit at home waiting until you feel like making an appearance."

Owen smiles, catching me off guard.

I swear he has mood swings. He can go from pissy to happy in two seconds. "What's so funny? You're giving me the creeps."

Steve chuckles.

Owen immediately scowls in his direction. "You said home."

Oh, crap. I did. How long have I been calling this place home? But it really does seem that way.

Owen reaches over, touching my arm. "Look, I'm sorry.

Someone came to me with a problem this morning, and I got delayed."

His kindness catches me off-guard. My anger thaws slightly until Rose slips into the vacant seat beside him.

She places her head on his shoulder, looking up at him. "Hey, baby. I've been looking for you all morning."

I jump up, ready to get out of here. After our kisses last night, I can't stand the thought of him with someone else. But, of course, this would happen. They are all the same.

Owen captures my hand, not letting me leave, and stands up beside me.

Rose glowers at our joined hands.

Steve's expression morphs into shock.

Owen wraps his arm around my waist, pulling me closer. "All right, Rose, it's time to clear the air. I'm not into you and definitely don't want to court you."

Everyone is watching and I realize what he's doing. If he were a dog, I'd be peed on right now. However, I can't make myself leave the comfort of his arms.

"Ariah and I are courting. Please, be aware," he stares directly at Steve, "that we are exclusive, and if anyone tries to interfere, there will be consequences. Does everyone understand?"

Steve nods, and Rose huffs, standing up.

She looks directly at me and walks over, whispering into my ear, "It's not over. Better watch your back."

I swear, she's a clone of Elizabeth, and there is already one too many of her. Everyone goes back to eating their food and getting ready for the day. I tilt my head up, looking him in the eye. "Feel better now?"

He grins. "Yes, sure do. Killed two birds with one stone. Now, Steve and Rose shouldn't be a problem, and everyone else has been warned. I think we should both be happy about that."

I snort and grab my plate, heading to the garbage area. I put up my dirty plates and head out the door, Owen following behind. I'm surprised he's with me. "Aren't you going to eat?"

At that moment, Jacob walks up.

Owen looks over. "Hey, do you mind bringing me something to eat to the training grounds? Mother's waiting for us."

Jacob grunts his acknowledgment, and Owen takes my hand again, leading me toward the forest.

I glance back at Jacob who's walking into the dining hall. "Does he ever say more than a few words?"

Owen tugs my hand again. "He tries not to, but every now and then, he's required to talk."

I chuckle and shake my head. It really is nice being out and a part of the forest, and to be fair, it's even better having him right beside me. Even though I'm trying not to get too attached, my heart seeks him out despite his jerkish tendencies.

My heart feels light for the first time in months. We walk in silence, but it's comforting, as if we've been doing it for years.

When we break through the clearing, Willow is already there and smiles when we approach. "What do we have here?"

"Oh, Mother, don't act surprised. You've been telling me to do this from the very beginning."

Why would his mother want us together? "What?"

She snorts, looking at me. "Ha, it's true, but you both are stubborn and still have a ways to go. So, when did you find out that I'm his mother?"

"Oh, Mer let it slip the other day."

Willow's eyebrows raise. "She lets you call her that?"

Why do people keep asking me that? "Well, yeah. Wait, I don't think I've actually called her by name. Isn't it Mer?"

Owen laughs again, and even though it's the second time, it's still as startling as the first time. He's truly gorgeous, especially when his green eyes light up like that, and his smile lights a fire in my soul. "No, Ariah, her name is Meredith. Only her family and close friends call her Mer."

"Oh, well, I'll make sure to call her Meredith, then."

Willow claps her hand. "Enough of this idle talk. We need to get on training. The war will start soon."

I just stay quiet. Asking her to explain herself will only result in more riddles. I'm tired of them and just want to get acclimated to my power. Ever since coming here, my power and I are finally becoming one. We are more in sync than ever, and it's not acting crazy on me anymore.

She has me run through some drills, and for once, I don't make Owen go away. In fact, it seems right for him to be here, like I'm more centered and connected. I now can make a tornado and add water or fire into the mix. It's challenging but can be done. It just drains me a little. After we practice with various exercises of shielding and power orbs, Willow turns to me.

"It's time to test you." She takes off deeper into the forest, and Owen and I follow. We walk a while, and the trees here are not as vibrant. A little while longer, and trees are nearly rotted with decay. This is where she stops, turning to me.

Owen stops a few steps back. "Willow, are you sure about this? It may be too soon."

"Shush, boy. We may let you lead most of the time, but don't forget who is truly in charge here," she chastises.

She whips her green eyes back to me. "I want you to channel your power here and see how the trees respond."

She expects me to ask more questions, but I've done this before. Without hesitation, I close my eyes and channel my power into the ground. I push it out as fast as possible, wanting to help the plants and animals that need to live here.

After a few moments, someone gasps. I'm not sure who, because I'm still focusing on my task. I'm not sure how much time has passed, but something nudges me in the back. I slowly open my eyes and turn to find Ares there, paying sole attention to me.

Owen's mouth has dropped open. "He's touching her."

Finding his comment odd, I open my mouth to say something, but suddenly I feel as if it's a chore to stand. I stumble and begin to fall, but Ares dips down, letting me land on his back. Oh, man, I used a lot more of my power than I realized. I feebly throw my leg around him, mounting him the best I can, and he rises. I'm slumped forward, with my head on his neck and my arms dangling down. However, right before I close my eyes to drift to sleep, I look out to where I had been standing and the rotted trees are back to a healthy brown bark with dark green leaves. They have been healed. Then, I crash into a deep slumber.

⚜

Owen's voice infiltrates my consciousness. "I can't believe she did that."

"What happened?" Oh, when did Mer join us?

I can hear sounds and conversations, but I'm not at all

aware. I open my eyes and find that I'm dreaming again and can actually see myself slumped over Ares. We are at the town's border, and Meredith is with us, heading back toward the village.

Mer checks my face and touches my arm. "Mother, is she all right?"

Willow comes over and pats Meredith's shoulder. "She's fine, dear, and Owen, don't fret. She's stronger than I realized, and she'll continue to strengthen, especially when everything has been completed. Mer, please, run and get some of the rejuvenating herbs. She really doesn't need it since she's so powerful, but it will help her bounce back a little faster."

Without any additional encouragement, Meredith runs off in search of the medicine.

Owen's face is pinched with worry. "Mother, how did she heal all those plants? I would never have thought that was possible. Is she going to be okay? I can't have her hurt."

I want to reach out and touch him, to let him know I'm okay. However, there is no way for me to do that.

Willow glances up in my direction, once again appearing like she knows I'm there. "Son, she'll be fine, but I'm glad you are starting to realize how much you care. She is meant to be one of us."

He gazes at me, his eyes soft, and brushes his fingertips against my cheek. "I can't even deny it anymore. I won't let her go."

For the first time ever, I think that a man I care about might be telling the truth. Have I found someone who will truly fight for me?

Someone is holding my hand, and I crack my eyes open to find Owen there. I try to sit up, but he's leaning over me, keeping me in place.

He gives me a small smile. "Stay right here. Don't get up yet. You used a lot of power. Let me get some of the rejuvenating herbs for you to drink. I'll be right back."

I look around and realize that I'm in a bed but not at my home. Where the hell am I?

Mer's voice rings out from across the room. "Calm down, princess. They brought you to my house. Don't worry about a soiled reputation."

She comes into view and sits down beside me with a sweet smile. "I'm glad you are okay. We were kind of worried, even though Mother insisted you'd be fine."

My voice is barely there. "Thanks." I clear my throat, trying to get it to come back.

Owen comes back into the room with a glass. I take it from him greedily and down the warm mixture. It soothes my throat, and immediately, some of my power sparks back to life. Maybe this stuff really does work.

He sits down on the edge of the bed. "Feel better?"

I nod. "Yes, thank you. I didn't realize how wiped I was."

"Yeah, you were a goner." He moves and rubs his fingers lightly across my cheek. "I can't believe the stallion came out to help you."

Oh, right. I forgot my grey friend was there. "Oh, Ares? Yeah, he seems to know when I need him."

Owen's face goes slack, and his jade eyes pierce mine. "Wait, you've seen him before and even named him?"

"Yeah, what's the big deal? Meredith's seen him before with me."

Owen's face turns cold, and he glares at his sister. "What's she talking about?"

Mer sighs and shifts around. "I may have found him with her each time I located her in the woods."

His face is livid. "What? And you didn't tell me?"

Mer sags back in her chair. "Owen, you didn't even want her here. If I'd told you that, you would have struggled with her being here more."

Why would he struggle with me being here even more? "What does Ares have to do with anything?"

Owen takes a deep breath, trying to calm down. "It just means you are very important to us... to me... Don't worry about it, okay? We can talk when you're more like yourself."

I want to argue, but he's right. I'm still extremely exhausted. I look out the window and realize its dusk, and I'm starving. My stomach growls at just that moment.

Meredith laughs and walks out the bedroom door. "I'll go grab us some dinner. Someone must be hungry."

Owen chuckles then moves closer to me on the bed. Concern is etched all over his face, and thankfully, he leans down to place a kiss on my lips. "Will you please stop scaring me?"

I tilt my head. "Scaring you?"

"Yes, stop running away and using too much of your power." He plays with a strand of my hair that has fallen out. "I can't protect you if you don't let me."

"I don't need your protection. Every time someone 'protects' me, I wind up hurt and betrayed. I am going to learn how to protect myself."

He sighs but surprises me by nodding his head in understanding. "I agree, you need to protect yourself, but I hope that, one day, I'll gain your trust enough so you're willing to rely on me as well." As soon as he's done with the sentence, he kisses me more, making my brain murky and my body warm all over.

After some time, someone knocks on the door. Mer's pleading voice pierces my ears. "Dear goodness, please, stop making out in my bed. That's my brother, princess. I don't want to be thinking of this when I lay down to sleep at night."

Oh, no. Please tell me she didn't catch us kissing.

Owen looks at me with a tender smile on his face. I really enjoy this side of him.

Mer comes over and snaps her fingers in between our gazes, demanding our attention. "All right, you're not eating in my bed. I refuse to sleep on crumbs. Owen, help your girl up and into the kitchen where we can all eat together."

Owen scoops me up in his arms.

I squeal. "Hey, I can walk myself."

He leans so he's talking in my ear. "But what fun is that?"

His closeness combined with his warm breath in my ear has my body responding in ways I'm not expecting. Being alone with him is not a good idea anytime in the near future.

He plops me down on one of the seats, and he sits next to me while Mer takes the chair across from me. I look down and fall a little in love with her. She filled my plate up to the max, and I'll wind up eating every morsel. We all sit in comfortable silence, enjoying our meal.

Why do all our meals come from the dining hall? Smiley sometimes eats at his house. I glance up. "Do you guys ever cook?"

Mer pauses, answering around a large mouthful of food. "Yeah, sometimes."

Owen laughs so hard, he chokes on a piece of food.

She sticks her tongue out at her brother. "Serves you right."

He takes a sip of water and clears his throat. He looks at me with a very serious look. "No, she can't."

Mer scowls at him. "Shut it, Owen. Just because it winds up charred doesn't mean anything. You can scrape the burnt pieces off, and it tastes just fine."

I laugh, but this also makes me miss Logan terribly. We used to banter just like this. I hope he and Claire are doing well and enjoying their time together.

Owen reaches out, rubbing my arm and giving me a wink.

I don't know who this person is sitting next to me, but I like him a lot better than the first version I met. "I was just curious because, apparently, Steve sometimes cooks his meals at home rather than eating at the dining hall."

Owen sours up at this comment, but his sister ignores him. "Yes, the villagers sometimes do. If one of their close friends hunts and kills something, but it's not big enough to share with the whole village, they will just share with their friends and cook at their house. That happens on occasion, but more often than not, they eat with us."

"I guess that makes sense."

We fall silent as we finish our meals. The food is delicious and tastes more similar to Agrolon's meals than Orlon's. It must be because they hunt and grow fresh vegetables here.

The decaying trees come back into my mind. What caused that? They are still in the middle of the forest, so a neighboring kingdom wouldn't affect it. And even though the Noslons live close by, they are so ingrained in nature that it couldn't be due to them.

Figuring I'll have more luck talking to Willow instead of

Owen and Meredith, I keep my mouth shut. I'll ask her and Owen tomorrow when we meet up for training. If I remember right, I did help revive the forest, so hopefully, that took care of the problem.

Soon, we are all done, and I stand up, wanting to go home. I'd love a shower and to crawl into bed. Meredith waves distracted with cleaning up, and Owen walks me home.

When we get to my door, he reaches up, caressing the side of my face. "Night, princess."

He bends down for a kiss. My mind stops working, and I lean in, deepening our kiss. He pulls back and gives me a wink.

"I'll be here first thing in the morning. Nothing will distract me this time." He winks and disappears into the dark.

Chapter Eighteen

The pounding on the door startles me awake. What the heck is going on? I jump out of bed and open the door without thinking of my appearance.

To my horror, Owen is there and totally taking in my disheveled state. He tilts his head and gives me one of his rare smiles. "I take it that I woke you up?"

I roll my eyes, and he slips past me, entering my home. "Oh, please come on in."

He is already sitting on my couch and glances my way. "Thanks. I'll just make myself at home."

I move toward the stairs to go up to my room so I can get ready, when he stands and captures my arm. "You feeling okay? Last night took a lot out of you."

The concern in his eyes is a little shocking, but my heart warms. "Yeah, I'm fine. Apparently, I needed some sleep. I'll hurry up, so we can get breakfast. I'm starving. If you don't want to wait for me, that's fine."

He touches my cheek and bends to graze his lips with mine. "I'm fine waiting. Take your time."

I head to my room to get ready with my lips still tingling. A small smile spreads across my face, and I hurry to get dressed. When I take a quick glance in the mirror, I'm reminded that all of the red has faded from my hair. It's back to its normal jet-black color. Maybe standing out isn't such a bad thing.

I pull my hair up into a ponytail and put on one of my new sets of black clothing and leather shoes. When I head back out, Owen glances up.

"You know, you're just as pretty when you first wake up as you are now, dressed and ready."

How do I respond to this? I know that can't be the case.

He snickers. "Come on, princess. Let's get you something to eat."

He takes my hand, and we walk over to the dining hall to start our day. As soon as we walk in, the room goes quiet, and I glance up.

Mer is grinning, sitting at their usual table, while Rose has to be thinking of ways to kill me.

I'm about to drop his hand, but Owen holds on tighter, refusing to let go.

He glances down at me, resolved. "They are going to have to get used to seeing us like this eventually."

Well, he wasn't joking about us being together. A stupid grin fills my face, and I walk over to the buffet and look at him. "I'm sorry, but I need food. I require my hand back."

He shakes his head, trying to hold back a smile.

Of course, he wouldn't want anyone to see him happy.

He lets my hand go, and I immediately attack the food. After loading up my plate, I head to my usual table.

Owen walks in front, cutting me off. "Hey, Ariah. We sit over here."

Not wanting to make a scene, I head over there, but really don't want to be near Rose and Jacob. Owen has us positioned where I'm sitting in between him and Mer, with Rose in front of him and Jacob in front of me.

Rose huffs loudly when I sit down, but everyone ignores her.

Jacob is quiet, like always, taking his time eating.

Mer is excited over something. She's fidgeting all over the place. "It's about time you two became official. The whole tension thing you have going on is... interesting."

Rose huffs and flips her hair. "Oh, please, Meredith. He'll be over her in a minute. He's only paying attention to her because she keeps running away."

Yeah, I can't stand her.

Mer sets down her fork and glances back up. "Poor Rose, you know Owen was just using you to try not to focus on her. Don't be so petty."

Rose's face turns nasty.

She is about to respond when Owen cuts her off. "Rose, get over it. You know we never worked. I did use you as a distraction, and I'm sorry, and everyone knows you're only interested in me because of my position."

Jacob smirks, and I open my mouth before I think through my words. "Hey, isn't Jacob like your second in command?"

Owen stops and gives me a funny look while Jacob tries to read me.

Mer answers me. "Yes, he is."

"So, problem solved. Rose, you should get Jacob to court you."

Mer and Owen laugh at my suggestion. Jacob's mouth drops open in shock, and Rose looks furious.

She jumps from her seat and storms out the door.

Mer is still laughing. "Oh, my goodness, yes. You have to court Rose"

Owen is laughing so hard that tears are falling down his cheeks, and Jacob's eyes are wide.

I really don't understand why my suggestion was so funny, but hey, I'll own it. I glance over at Jacob. "That's what you get for not talking."

Owen laughs harder, and Jacob arches an eyebrow. "Touché. But remember, two can play at this game."

"Bring it." I meet his challenging gaze.

"All right, that's enough. Don't stroke the beast. I'm not sure you know what you're getting yourself into," Owen interrupts, giving Jacob a warning look.

Jacob understands something that I've missed, but my food is getting cold. Delighted that Rose is gone, I tear into my meal, perfectly at ease.

Mer finishes and cleans up her stuff. "Ariah, when you have some time, do you want to come over? I have a few things I'd like to show you."

I just nod, because I have a large bite of food in my mouth.

She bounces on her feet, and heads toward the door. "Great. Come see me after your practice."

I look up and find that I'm the focus of Jacob's attention. "Something I can help you with?"

"Nope," he answers and goes back to being silent. We all finish, so we clean up our messes and head out the door.

Jacob pauses and looks at Owen. "You going to hunt today?"

Owen takes my hand. "Nope, I'm going with Ariah. Hope

you find something big that will really help out our food supplies."

It looks like Jacob wants to say something in response, but decides to bite his tongue instead. He gives me another assessing look, and I stand straighter. I refuse to cower to this man and am so tired of being bullied.

He sighs and turns to head on his merry way. I'm surprised to find that Owen watched the whole thing.

I glance down at our joined hands. "What's his problem?"

Owen gives me a tight smile. "Ariah, remember, we aren't used to outsiders. There's a very specific reason for that. Just give him some time; he's my best friend."

I nod, understanding that it's wise to not just trust someone right off. Haven't I learned that the hard way?

Owen lightly tugs my hand, and we finally arrive at the training area.

When we get closer, something alerts me that there are intruders. Obviously, Owen gets it, too, because he stiffens and steps slightly in front of me as if shielding me.

Willow appears from behind a tree with wide eyes. She places a finger to her lips.

Owen nods, and we turn to follow her back to the village.

As soon as we are safely back within our borders, Owen turns to his Mother. "What happened back there?"

She glances back to where we had just come from. "There were people out there, very close to our borders. Their intent was not very noble."

The key on my necklace flairs to life. Ever since I got here, it's been silent, almost like it was content to be back home, but obviously, it's awake now. Just like the first time I came to this village, there is an undeniable pull, leading me to the river.

JEN L. GREY

Owen's tone is urgent. "Ariah, where are you going?"

But I'm in such a trance-like state that I find I can't answer. I need to follow where this key is taking me. Something important is waiting for me.

Owen calls my name again, but Willow interrupts, "Let's follow her. Something is going on."

They are close on my heels, and I finally make it to the river and head toward the cave. Owen immediately steps in front of me. "You can't go there, Ariah. You'll get hurt."

I try to go around him, but he moves with me, blocking my destination. Without warning, my power spurs to life, knocking him out of my way.

It catches him off guard and he falls, but gets back on his feet.

I head for the cave again, and he throws a little power at me, knocking me slightly off-kilter. At the small attack, raw power like never before fills me. Willow gasps, and Owen's face transforms into awe.

Willow grabs Owen, pulling him to her side. "Move out of her way."

But he hesitates. "Mother, I can't."

She squeezes his hand. "It will be all right, trust me."

With him out of my way, I wander into the cave. The key pulses stronger, as if adding more power to the mix. What's amazing is, when I walk into the dark cave, it's actually not dark at all. Light is illuminated everywhere. Looking at the walls, there are symbols and pictures everywhere, telling a story.

As I take them all in, I'm amazed. It's like the prophecy we've been told for so long is displayed here for me to see, only in pictures.

Dark will prevail, and distrust will run rampant. With the

174

people unaware, an evil tyrant will arise. A corrupt kingdom will prevail until a second of Pearson ascends. Her unrivaled power will transcend after a bond is formed. Trials and tribulations will abound. Only then can she bring the light to the dark, with the power of three and a key.

An elaborate picture of all the kingdoms is displayed before me, each of them vibrant in color, with a circle connecting them all.

Right next to the images is another drawing of the same kingdoms, but they are covered in darkness with an X next to each entry point. For some reason, the West has a red eye positioned so it looks as if it's staring out at the viewer. I move so I can see the next picture.

This one is also of the kingdoms, only in gray instead of color, except the southernmost kingdom has a faint golden glow where the palace is located. Right beside that, it shows a girl with dark hair curled up on the ground in the fetal position. I can't see any details, but it's clear she's in pain. However, I can't focus, because the next drawing is calling my name.

Once again, it's of Knova, but the East has magic coming out of the picture. It's pure white with two joined circles, indicating a bond of some sort. The last picture has the same girl standing in the center of the kingdoms with an elaborate crown on her head. She has a man on both sides of her, and there's a key tied around her neck that looks a lot like the key I'm wearing.

Owen gasps. "What in Knova?"

I want to talk to him, but now that I've seen all the pictures, my key seems to be working its power again. I'm drawn to the very back corner of the cave. There appears to be a very dark crevasse, but somehow, I know it isn't.

Owen's voice is a warning. "Ariah…"

But Willow shushes.

When I get there, I fall down on my knees, and the light shines in the dark spot. There in the center, at the very bottom, where the cave meets the floor, there is a keyhole. I take the necklace off and lower the key to the ground, inserting it into the hole. I turn it and hear it click, and then the wall starts moving.

Owen is not happy. "What in the hell is going on?"

But I don't have time to answer him. When the wall is pushed all the way to the side, there is a wooden box sitting on the shelf. I pick it up, surprised that it's not as heavy as I was expecting, and I turn to look at Willow and Owen.

Owen inspects the box. "Okay, what is that?"

Now that I'm out of whatever spell I was under, I shrug. "I have no clue."

Willow touches the box. "Let's take it to her house."

Owen glances at his mother. "Why hers?"

Willow smacks him on the arm. "It was obviously meant for her. You can't take power items away from the intended owner. You'd just be asking for trouble."

We make it to the house quickly, where we all hover in the living room. There is a keyhole in the box as well, and I still have the key in my hand from where I took it off in the cave. I insert my key into the opening, and it fits perfectly, but it won't turn. What the hell?

Owen takes the key from me. "Is it jammed?"

Even when he uses his full strength, it won't budge.

Willow moves toward the door. "Obviously, she's not meant to open it yet. We will find out in due time. I think that's enough excitement for one day. I'm heading home." The door shuts behind her.

Owen looks at me, concern outlining his handsome face. "You scared me today."

Always complaining, isn't he? "I either scare, aggravate, or annoy you. Why do you keep me around?"

He shakes his head and chuckles. "Because you keep it interesting and make sure I'm on my toes. Not many people do that." He tugs me to him and kisses me on my lips. When he pulls back, he runs his fingers through my hair. "You were lit up like a firefly, but your glow was pure white. It was actually very beautiful. Even your eyes were glowing."

"Huh? What do you mean?" My eyes were glowing again?

He runs his nose against my neck. "In the cave. All that light in the cave was from you. I was petrified something was going to happen to you."

"I've been told I had a faint glow before, but it's usually when I use my powers." I close my eyes enjoying his attention.

He pulls back, his eyes on mine. "That girl in the picture, she looked a lot like you."

"Why do you say that? I couldn't see anything distinguishing."

He grimaces. "It's the feeling I got, but I would never want to see you in pain like that."

I snort hard. If he only knew.

He tenses and searches for something in my eyes. "What aren't you telling me, princess?"

I take a deep breath and sigh. "Owen, can we please just have fun? Haven't we dealt with enough today?"

He wants to push, I can tell, but stays quiet. "All right, but I will want those answers eventually. Let's go check on the hunters, especially since there were outsiders around the border."

I forgot all about that, and with how we are rushing, I can tell he's more worried than he's letting on. I follow as he takes off toward a side of the village I'd never ventured to before. We pass some older-looking houses and then stumble upon some fire pits and areas where meat is hanging up for cooking.

There is a large crowd of men gathered around, and as soon as they see Owen, they break apart and turn toward him.

Owen looks at each of them. "What's going on?"

Jacob steps out from the center. "Owen, there were some outsiders near our border. Luckily, we had finished the hunt for the day and were able to get back undetected. However, it was a large group. I've never seen a size that large near here. It's almost as if they are seeking us."

Alarm rings throughout me, knowing how important it is for the Noslons to go unnoticed. "Did you notice anything about them?"

At my question, people glance at each other and become quiet. No one answered me, but I'm not surprised.

Before I can say anything else, Owen puts his arm around my waist and looks at them expectantly. Maybe he isn't such a jerk after all.

Jacob takes a deep breath. "Yes, we did. They appeared to be armed guards, and the symbol on their shields looked like Agrolon's, but we aren't completely sure about that."

Oh, no. Why would Agrolon guards be looking for Noslon? My heart races, and I almost stumble backward.

However, Owen squeezes my waist as if to remind me that he is there. "All right, it looks like you all brought enough food back to last a while. No more hunting for the next week. Let's give these people time to stop looking for us and clear out. I'm glad each one of you is safe and was able to be discreet."

The crowd disperses, pleased that Owen was informed and they now have their orders.

Jacob walks over to us and looks at me. "Did you forget?"

What is he talking about? "Forget what?"

"Meredith is going to be disappointed if you don't show up."

Yikes. I forgot I promised that I would go over to her house. I wiggle out of Owen's grip and head back to the center of town. "See you later."

⚜

I knock on her door, and it opens within seconds.

Mer is smiling, motioning me inside. "Hey, Ari."

People usually aren't this excited to see me. I walk into the house and take a seat on her couch. "Hey."

She follows me in, her face excited. "Oh, I made some stuff I wanted you to see. We are having a party in a few weeks, and everyone always dresses up. Now that my brother is courting you, you have to be one of the best dressed. This is a huge deal, especially since Owen has always gone solo."

"He might want to still go solo. I wouldn't get my hopes up just yet." I bite my lip and look out the window, trying to school my expression. The thought of him going with Rose burns my belly.

"Oh, please. He is so smitten with you, it's almost ridiculous. Which is funny, because usually, girls fall all over him, but not you," she snickers.

She walks into her room and comes back with a handful

of dresses. Most are black, but there are some colorful options, which surprises me. She lays them out and puts her finger to her bottom lip, taking inventory. "Let's see... Is there anything that catches your fancy?"

I step beside her and look at the options. She pulls out a nude one that has clear straps and is fitted on top then tapers off slightly going down. It's actually a very pretty, simple dress. "Try this one on. I bet it will look good with your coloring, and it will give you something other than black to wear."

Pleased with what she's selected, I take a deep breath and change right there. My hands get clammy, but I'm determined to bury my demons. I change quickly into the dress, and she smiles at my appearance. "Perfect. That one is yours."

I smile and look at the dresses again. "Hey, Mer? Why is most of our clothing black?"

She glances at me. "Our clothing, huh? Well, it's because we don't have easy access to the colorful berries. They are near the borders of the other kingdoms, and we try to stay hidden. The black is easier to find and is actually more durable. Plus, it makes us look tough." She winks at me and pulls a red dress from the pile. "This one will be mine."

I leave her to her fun and quickly change back into my normal clothes. There is a knock at the door while I'm changing in the bedroom, and Mer walks out to answer it.

When I join them, I find that Owen is here. "Hey, princess. Having fun?"

I walk over and smack him on the arm. "Yup, having a grand time."

Mer glances at me, a sneaky look on her face. On, no. What is she going to do?

She nudges her brother on the arm. "Speaking of fun

times, you do plan on asking Ariah to go to the party with you, right?"

I groan. I can't believe she actually did that. Surely, he doesn't think I put her up to it. I'm about to speak, but Owen beats me.

He scowls at his sister, clearly not amused. "Of course, but I planned to do it when we were alone." He turns to me, "Ariah, I would love to escort you to the party."

I stand there and just look at him. He gets tense, rubbing his hands together. "Uh… is that a no?"

Wait, what? "What are you talking about?"

He sighs. "I asked if you would go to the party with me."

"Actually, you did not." I roll my eyes. "But, yeah. I'll go with you."

Mer laughs.

Owen takes a deep breath and puts a hand over his mouth. He closes his eyes. "You don't sound very happy about it."

Crap, I think I might have hurt his feelings. "Sorry, parties and I don't get along. Every one I've gone to has ended in a disaster. It's not you. It's me."

Mer smacks him on the arm. "Ha. How many times have you used that same phrase on someone?"

Her comment actually ticks me off. I don't want to think about him with other girls. Seeing him with Rose was enough to make me want to run away.

He groans at his sister's joke and takes my hand. "Hey, it's getting late. Want to go grab something to eat?"

That sounds like the best idea. I place my hand over my heart. "Food is always good with me."

Mer shakes her head. "All right, see you later. Hey, leave

the dress here. I mean, you'll be coming to get dressed here with me, so we can get ready together, right?"

Yeah, I don't have the heart to tell her no. "Uh, yeah, sure. That works."

She grins at my response, and Owen pulls me out of the doorway.

When we walk into the dining hall, the room is pretty much bare since we are early and missing the rush. We make our plates and eat quickly.

Afterwards, we head back to my home. Sitting in the living room is the unopened box. I really want to know what's inside of it, but it's not going to happen today.

Owen sits down on the couch, leaning over the box and inspecting it. "What do you think it is?"

I touch the key on my necklace. "I'm not sure, but the key fits perfectly."

He sits back and glances up at me. It's amazing that he's here in my home spending time with me. "Yeah, Willow said you'd be able to open it when it's time. I wonder when that will be?"

Wanting to forget about the box, I walk over and grab his hand. "Hey, want to go for a walk? I thought I'd seen all of the village, but I hadn't been where you took me with the hunters."

He grins up at me and stands. "Sure, let's go. I need to see what's going on anyway."

We head out, and I quickly realize that everyone is ending their day and heading for food. We walk past the fields and get close to the lake. When we reach the cave and water, I lay down, making myself at home.

He looks at me, confused. "What are you doing?"

"I just enjoy laying down out in nature. I don't know why,

but I've always loved it." I motion to the spot beside me. "Come join me."

He complies with my request, and we both look up at the sky. Dusk is ascending, and we lay together with our hands joined. After a while, I get up the nerve to ask him something that I've been wondering the whole time. "Do you have powers?"

He takes a deep breath. "Why would you ask that?"

"Because you deflected some of my power the other day, and it seemed as if you hit me with some today when my key was being crazy."

He bites his lips. "Yes."

I'm shocked, even though I shouldn't be. I mean, I speculated he did. "How is that possible?"

He looks over and taps me on the nose. "That is a story for another time. Only a handful of people know, so I'm trusting you not to tell anyone."

I get it, what he's doing. He truly let me in on a secret, but not all of it. I respect his decision, because I'm still an outsider, even though I'm starting to be a part of the group. "Fair enough."

He reaches over and puts his arm around my waist. The yearning starts up immediately at his touch. "You know, this really is nice. I'm all about the outdoors, but never take the time just to lay out here and enjoy the sky."

I gaze into his eyes, lost in his tender spell. "It's beautiful, especially out here. My power surges in moments like this, but not unpleasantly. I remember when I used to have a hard time with it, but now, I'm one with the power. It's peaceful in moments like this."

He looks at me. "You really are different."

"I'm tired of trying to blend in. It's never really worked before anyway."

He reaches his hand out and tilts my face toward him. "That's a very good thing."

As soon as those words are out, his lips are on mine. My body is instantly on fire. Everywhere he's touching causes my body to buzz, and my brain gets hazy. I never want to stop kissing him, and I'm desperate for more. We are both in a frenzied state, and he rolls over on top of me. My hands find their way into his hair, and his hands roam down toward my belly.

There is laughter right above us. Willow's voice makes me flinch. "Well, it sure seems like you two are getting along better."

Owen's hands stop, and he rolls beside me, keeping an arm around me.

I want to move away from him, but for some reason, I can't. My body won't allow it. I just wish I could disappear. I can't believe his mother caught us!

She smirks at us, almost like it's an inside joke.

I fidget and look down at the ground. Will this night ever end?

He tightens his hold on me, and I bury my face in his shoulder. "What can I help you with, Mother?"

Did he just call her mother? That's odd. He normally uses her first name.

"I wanted to check on you two. I figured you'd be down here either fighting or canoodling."

I'm very perplexed. I move my mouth to Owen's ear. "What's canoodling?"

He bursts out laughing. His whole body is shaking.

Willow takes a step back. "Well, Owen, I haven't seen you this carefree since you were a boy."

This sobers him up, but he still has me locked in an embrace.

Wanting to escape from his mother's watchful gaze, I move his arm and stand. It is so difficult. It's almost like Owen is a magnet, pulling me to him.

He turns his gaze on me. "Hey, what do you think you're doing?"

I raise an eyebrow. "Going home. It's getting dark, and I'm tired."

Disappointment fills his eyes, but he gets to his feet.

Willow shakes her head. "Having trouble letting someone else be in charge?"

He glares at her but makes his way over to me. "I'll walk you home. Goodnight, Mother."

"Night, kids. Owen, you'll be training with Ariah tomorrow."

He stiffens, but then takes a quick breath and relaxes. We head toward the village, and the farther away we get from Willow, the more he truly goes back to being less guarded.

I get to my door, and he looks at me. "Aren't you going to invite me in?"

I laugh, knowing that it would not be a wise thing to do. "I would, but I don't think that would be smart for either of us." He looks confused, which causes me to chuckle. "You really are used to getting your way."

For the first time ever, a sheepish look crosses his face. "Well… okay, yeah."

I giggle. "Well, that stops here and now. Goodnight, Owen. I'll see you in the morning."

I turn to walk in, but he grabs my hand, pulling me around so my back is to the door. His lips are on me immediately, and the yearning returns full force. I'm about to go back under whatever spell we have, but I push him away in time. "As much as I enjoy this, I have a big day tomorrow. See you."

He stands there in shock, truly not expecting me to do that. I shut the door in his face. He must have regained some of his composure, though, because he yells, "I'll pick you up for breakfast."

Chapter Nineteen

S omeone sits on my bed, startling me awake.

Mer's voice pounds in my ears. "Good morning."

I pull the covers over my face. "How in the hell did you get in here?"

Mer tugs the covers back down. "Oh, wow. Someone does not wake up in a chipper mood."

I glare at her. "No, I'm not chipper until after my first cup of coffee. Once again, what are you doing?"

She's not intimidated at all. She actually grins. "Oh, well, since our family is over this place, we have keys to every house. So, I am super excited about something I found and need to show you right away."

"Mer, you can't just come into someone's house. What is wrong with you?" I put a pillow over my face.

"I've never done it before. Don't worry."

"You just did it to me." I throw the pillow at her.

She catches the pillow and tosses it aside. "Yeah, but you're different. Look." She holds out some chocolate.

JEN L. GREY

She's insane. I hold my hands up and close my eyes. "Did you seriously just wake me up because of chocolate?"

"Well, yeah. I've only ever had it once and thought we could share." Her smile falters, losing some of her enthusiasm.

Now, I am officially a jerk. "Sorry, Mer. I'd love to have a piece."

Her smile comes back, and she breaks off a piece and hands it over.

I pop it in my mouth and find it's the worst piece of chocolate I've ever had in my life, but Mer doesn't appear affected.

"This is so amazing," she mumbles around a huge mouthful.

I have to grin at her enthusiasm.

She swallows. "How are you not enjoying this as much as me?"

"Well, honestly, I ate a lot of it growing up. The palace always had some around."

She stiffens at my explanation. She opens her mouth to speak, but there is a large knock at the door.

I jump up, eager to get away for some reason, and open the door without thinking. Owen stands there, looking better than ever before, and I'm here with my pajamas and bed head. Great.

He smirks at me and takes a step toward me. He pulls me into his arms and has his mouth on mine within seconds.

Mer must have followed me downstairs, because her voice pierces across the room. "Oh my gosh! Really?"

Owen pauses, and I pull away. In less than twenty-four hours, both his mother and sister have caught us kissing.

Owen looks at her. "What in the hell are you doing here,

Mer?" Then his eyes settle back on me. "And why do you taste like chocolate?"

She walks over to us. "I came to visit Ariah. I got my hands on some chocolate and wanted to share." She pushes her finger into his chest. "You're not the only one who likes being around her, you know."

Before this can get any weirder, I interrupt. "Okay, let me go change. I hear breakfast calling my name."

I run out of the room into nice peaceful solitary. I'm not a coward, just socially awkward. Wait, why would that make me feel any better? I quickly change and find them both sitting on the couch when I return to the living room.

I still can't meet Mer's eyes, so my eyes find the door. "You guys ready?"

Owen gives me a big grin.

Mer just smirks while shaking her head.

He stands up, taking my hand and pulling me toward the door. "Hungry, princess?"

"Yes. Also, I hear a large pot of coffee calling my name!"

We walk into the dining hall, and my belly rumbles. I grab myself a plate and quickly load it up before grabbing a huge cup of steaming coffee.

Owen's already at the table, sitting with Jacob.

I walk over and plop beside him, then take a large sip of heaven from my mug.

As soon as Mer sits down, I announce, "We need to talk about boundaries."

Owen perks up. "What are you talking about? You better not be trying to get rid of me. It's not happening."

I grin and bite my lip. I lean in and kiss his cheek quickly. Focus, Ari. There have more important things to discuss. I point at Mer. "She let herself into my home this morning while I was sleeping. I woke up to her sitting on my bed."

Jacob laughs, and I turn my glare on him. "Watch it."

He snickers more, and Owen puts his arm around my waist, drawing me near.

I attempt to push away. "Hey, don't try to distract me."

He smiles, and I can't help but stare. He really is the most handsome man I've ever seen.

Mer whispers to Jacob. "She sure told him."

Jacob chuckles, and I realize I've been caught. Making a point, I turn my body away from Owen and focus just on my coffee. As long as I have caffeine, everything will be all right in my world.

After everyone finishes eating, I jump up, more eager than normal for my training.

Owen grabs my hand, leading me back outside.

Jacob follows us. "Hey, Owen, let's hurry and go check on the hunters."

Owen turns and looks back at him. "Not happening. I'm going with Ariah this morning. Let me know what I miss at dinner tonight."

Jacob doesn't look pleased, but nods.

We say our goodbyes, and Owen and I march to our place in the forest. He seems uneasy as we walk out here, but we don't hear anyone nearby this time.

Willow is waiting for us in the opening.

He looks around the perimeter. "Should we not be near the borders?"

She shakes her head. "I think we are fine, and honestly, for what needs to be done, it's best if we stay out here."

Oh, that sounds interesting. "What are we doing?"

"You and Owen are going to practice your power together."

Owen gasps, and I am relieved that it's all been confirmed. "Are you…"

"Oh, shush. She already knows, and the two of you are together." Willow motions between him and me. "Were you planning on hiding it for the rest of your life?"

What? Did she just marry me off? Focus, Ariah. That's not the important part. "So, you have more than I've seen?"

Owen is tense, but to his credit, he answers me. "Yes, and I was going to tell you. I just wanted more time."

Not wanting to dwell on his admission, I turn to Willow. "All right, what do you want us to do?"

She clears her throat. "I want you to use your powers together and try to connect to one another."

"What? Are you crazy? It's dangerous to try to connect to one another," Owen snaps, anger in his eyes.

She scowls in his direction. "It can be, but will you just try?"

"Fine, but if she gets hurt, you'll have to answer for it," he growls.

Okay, so I guess we are doing this.

He turns to me and takes both of my hands, causing my power to instantly spring to life. "You ready?"

I nod and close my eyes. I focus on my power that answers willingly, pushing it out toward him, asking for it to connect. The buzzing that's always present becomes stronger. Before long, it seems as if a piece of him is inside my mind. It's similar to what I had with Logan but a whole lot stronger. I can tell what he feels, hear what he's thinking. Our powers merge in such a way that I can't tell where his begins and mine ends. Suddenly, pain engulfs my wrist, and I

JEN L. GREY

cry out. I open my eyes and see that Owen is holding his wrist, as well.

He reaches out to me. "Are you okay?"

I nod and look down at my wrist. I'm stunned. How in the world did I get this tattoo? It's the bird and thorns from my key. However, the family crescent is missing.

Owen looks down at his wrist. *"No way. That's impossible."*

I look at him. "What's impossible?"

He glances at me with a weary look.

Since he's ignoring me, I reach over and flip his wrist, so I can see the underside. My heart skips a beat when I realize he has the same tattoo as me.

His tone is frantic. *"What? You have the same tattoo?"*

My mouth drops open. "How did you know that?"

He gives me a confused look. "You just said it. How else would I know?"

I am about to freak out when Willow comes over and grabs both of our wrists. "Amazing. You are truly bonded and now bound to one another."

Owen grabs her hand. "Mother! What did you do?"

Is it odd that, right now, out of everything, I find him calling her Mother the strangest of all? It's always been Willow until recently.

He glares at me. "Really, princess? Out of everything, you're focusing on that?"

"Get out of my head." I project in my head, directing it toward him.

He puts his hands on his head. "Damn it, Ariah. You don't have to scream."

Willow laughs and rubs her hands together while shaking her head.

He redirects his attention to her, relieving me from his moaning.

"Calm down, Owen. This was meant to happen. I've been watching you. Seeing how you reacted to her the first time you met told me everything."

He is getting riled back up again.

She holds her hand out, stopping him. "You both are drawn to each other and are each powerful in your own right, especially Ariah. Your powers call to one another, wanting to connect. Don't you find it strange that you never could take a girl seriously until her?"

He takes a deep breath. "Fine, I'll admit that I'm drawn to her."

"More than drawn, dear boy. You almost went ballistic that day she came here to live." She raises an eyebrow. "How'd you know she was out in the woods with no home?"

He grabs me around the waist, and there's a hardness to his face which surprises me. "I knew something was wrong. I had a dream that she was racing from the Orlon Kingdom with nowhere to go. I saw a bear try to attack her, and then I woke up, needing to locate her."

My eyes pop open. "You saw the bear attack me?"

Concern outlines his face. "Yes, did it really happen?"

"Yes, the day before I came here. Sam was going to come find me and ask for the ring he gave me back. The king made him realize that there was no future between us because of my home kingdom. I knew I had to go before he found me. The last time something like that happened, I was thrown over a balcony."

I've never seen him this angry. A vein is bulging on the side of his neck. "What the hell are you talking about? Are you talking about Prince Samuel from Orlon? What kingdom are you from?"

How do I fix this? I don't want this to be a big deal. "Yes, my home kingdom is Agrolon. The king threw me over the balcony. Prince Samuel saved me."

His body stiffens. Apparently, I didn't do a good job downplaying the situation.

Willow steps next to me, smiling while putting her hand on her son's shoulder. "You're from Agrolon? We always thought you were from Orlon. Why did your king push you off the balcony, and how did you survive?"

"Well, see, I had a relationship with the prince…"

"From Orlon?" he growls.

I shudder, not wanting to go on, but this needs to come out. "Well, yes, but with the Agrolon prince first."

His eyes widen and he breathes erratically. "Are you freaking serious?"

Is he being serious? "Oh, stop being dramatic. It was before you."

Willow glares at him. "Please, ignore my son and tell us everything."

"Well, Nick and I had been good friends ever since we were kids, despite his father's hatred. We naturally fell into a relationship when we both got older, but his father wanted him to marry my sister. He refused, and long story short, his father threw me over the balcony to get me out of the way, and Nick let him."

Her face creases with confusion. "Why did his father hate you? Why were you even living in the palace?"

I don't want to tell them this. I'm sure this will change everything, but they've helped me and deserve the truth. I take a deep breath. "My sister is the Savior, and they wanted her tied to them for control. The king couldn't stand my older brother and me."

I have Owen's full attention, but his face is unreadable.

Willow is trying to be calm and get all the facts. "Your sister is the Savior? How'd you escape?"

"Yes, Emerson is my sister. My trainer, Lydia, somehow knew this was going to happen, and she helped slow my fall. She's one of the most powerful women in our kingdom. Her sister went to get Sam, and he took me to Orlon, his kingdom. But then the Orlon king made an arrangement with Agrolon, so Sam has to marry Princess Elizabeth of Agrolon. The king wanted Sam to get the ring back from me that he proposed with, and Sam agreed. That's when I knew I had to leave, and that's how I wound up here that day. I was on my way here with Pierce, one of the Orlon guards who offered to protect me."

Owen reaches out and flips my wrist over. His tone possessive, "You do realize you're mine now. They can't have you."

I glare at him. "I'm not anyone's, so quit acting that way."

His breaths are raged and his nostrils flare. "Like hell, you're not."

"Oh, calm down, Owen. That's no way to talk to your soulmate. She is yours, but she is not your property, so it'd do you good to learn some manners and respect." She scowls at him. "You started this off faster with the little blood promise you did with her anyway, so leave it be."

"She's mine," he grumbles, but I don't pay any attention. He's being the version of himself that I'm not a huge fan of.

Not wanting to deal with him any longer, I turn and head back to the village.

Owen stares at me in disbelief. "Where do you think you're going?"

"Away from you." I glance back at him, flipping my hair. "I'm tired of dealing with your grumpy attitude."

I keep going, not wanting him to catch up. I need some time to myself, so I can process everything. Having told them my story brings some relief, but at the same time, it brings up bad memories.

Also, I'm now bound to him? I'm not sure how I feel about that. I love him, but… What? Do I love him? My steps falter. I do, but I don't like that I wasn't given a choice. Taking a deep breath, I make my way back to the village and find Jacob at my door. Like this day could get any stranger.

"Hey, you. Owen is still back there with Willow." I point to the woods and move around him to open the door.

He clears his throat. "I want to talk to you, actually, so I'm glad he's preoccupied."

Unease creeps between us, but I open the door and motion for him to come in. "All right, what's up?"

He cracks a smile. "I do like that about you. Straight to the point. Not many girls are like that. Look, I've never seen Owen and Meredith like this before, and you're an outsider. What are your intentions?"

I can't help but laugh, but I'm truly happy that he cares about them enough to have this uncomfortable conversation with me. "Well, I have no intentions. It just kind of happened. Look, I'm not going anywhere. I'm done running away. To be honest, even if I wanted to, I have nowhere to go. I promise, I will never intentionally hurt either of them, and you can bring all kinds of pain on me if I do."

His shoulders relax from all the tension. I hadn't noticed how concerned he'd been. Oh, well. Not my problem.

Owen breezes through my door and comes to an abrupt halt when he sees Jacob standing there. Annoyance is clear on his face. He walks over to me, wrapping his arm around my waist. "What's going on?"

Jacob winces, obviously ready to be torn in two, but I can't let a concerned friend take the fall like that. "Oh, in my mad rush to get back here, I stumbled, and Jacob was there and saw it all. He wanted to make sure I was okay before going back to the hunting grounds."

Owen gives me an amused look. "I'll act like I believe that since you're covering for him." He then points at Jacob. "Did you get what you needed? This is the only time this will be tolerated."

Jacob shakes his head and smirks. "Yeah, I did. I'll see you at dinner."

When the door shuts behind him, Owen turns to me. "What did he say?"

"He just wanted to make sure I'll stick around."

"Like you even have a choice at this point. We're bonded. I'll come find you," he vows, pulling me closer to him.

My heart warms, and my pulse quickens. His statement should scare me, but it actually comforts me. Then, his lips are on mine, and just like that, all my anger with him evaporates. We both lose track of time.

I have no clue how long we've been kissing, but there is a loud knock at my door right before it's pushed open. I pull apart from Owen, and he groans in frustration.

Mer just breezes in like this is her place. "Hey, Mother is looking for you two." She halts and takes in our appearance.

I lick my lips and notice how swollen they are.

She smiles brightly, clearly amused. "What ya doing?"

She's caught us twice in one day. How am I ever going to live this down?

Owen doesn't seem to mind her teasing. "Mer, I'd like to get back to what I was doing, so can you just leave?"

I push on his chest. "Hey, I told you she has boundary issues."

Mer puts a hand on her hip. "It's okay. I'm delightful."

Does she think this is okay? "What does that have to do with anything? You can't just walk into people's homes because you're delightful."

Owen bursts out laughing, and I scowl in his direction. Great, now he's laughing even harder.

Mer looks at him like he's grown an extra head. "It's so weird seeing you like this, Owen. I mean, I'm happy for you, but sometimes, I miss my brooding brother."

"Thanks, Mer. Now scram." He bends down and captures my lips again.

"Nope, not going to happen. Now, stop kissing." She walks over and gets right in our faces.

It's an effective mood-killer.

Owen pulls back and narrow his eyes. "Are you being serious?"

She puts her hands on her hips. "Mother wants us. She says we need to talk."

Owen grumbles, and we get up to follow Mer to wherever Willow is. We approach the lake, and I find her sitting there on a blanket with her eyes closed.

Mer plots on the ground next to her. "Mother, I found them."

Willow opens her eyes.

Oh, her eyes glow, too. "Your eyes… they say my eyes do that, too."

She blinks and they turn to her normal blue shade. "I know, dear. You told us some of your story, and now it's time for us to share with you, as well. War is coming, and we need to be prepared. It's always been near, but I feel it in the air now. Your bond has escalated it."

Owen gives her a strange look. "What are you talking about?"

"Dear boy, you don't know everything." She reaches out and pats his arm.

She stands and walks over to the water, bending to dip her fingers in it. "As you know, men are not supposed to hold power, but Owen is an exception to the rule. I'm one of the most powerful women around, except for you, Ariah."

Owen wants answers, but I've learned that if you push, Willow will actually withhold more information. I've learned now to have patience when it comes to learning things. *"Let her finish, please."* I direct toward him. Surprisingly, he closes his mouth and squeezes my hand.

"That's one reason why we put up barriers and hid our village. If outsiders realize that our king has powers, they will either fear us or try to use us. Unfortunately, Owen and Meredith's dear, sweet father passed away when they were young, and all the attention was on Owen. We couldn't let the other kingdoms know that a child was leading us. We had to hide to survive, which turned out to be the best thing for us. Instead of abusing the lands, we had to nurture the earth and learn to bond with our surroundings in order to survive. We couldn't buy produce and meat from Agrolon, or silks from Orlon, unless we came out of hiding, which wasn't an option. However, the time is coming to change. War is brewing. Someone in the West is building an army to defeat Agrolon and their Savior. They have engineers that are building weapons and secure housing. They are turning to death and destruction with its own kind of evil power."

Owen gives her a peculiar expression. "How in Knova do you know this, Mother?"

"I have my ways, and be thankful I do. For now, I'm tired and ready to get some dinner then go home to bed. We have a big day of training tomorrow." She kisses Owen on the forehead and hugs me. She makes her way to Mer. "Behave." She kisses her, too, and heads back to the village.

Mer turns to us. "What the hell was that? We're going to war?"

Owen shrugs. "Mer, I have no clue, but I don't like that she's hiding stuff from me."

"Well, welcome to the club. I've been left in the dark most of my life. It's nice to have some company." I try to tease, but it falls short. Have I mentioned my social skills?

Owen just shakes his head at me with a smirk. "Just be glad you're nice to look at, princess."

Mer covers her ear with her hands. "Oh, dear, I do not want to hear this kind of mushy talk. Mother had the right idea about getting something to eat." She pulls me away from Owen and intertwines her arm in mine.

I laugh, thinking she must feel the same way I did when Claire and Logan started dating. I wonder how they are doing.

Within a few minutes, we are walking into the dining hall, and, as always, our table is vacant.

Rose, of course, is now sitting at a different table. However, she snarls as soon as she notices me.

I ignore her and fill up my plate.

Mer laughs. "If looks could kill."

Owen comes up next to me and loads up his plate, "What's so funny?"

Mer glances back at Rose. "Rose totally wants to kill Ariah here. You sure rocked her world."

Okay, I get it. She's interested in him. "Okay, enough. I don't want to hear about him rocking anyone's world."

Owen gives me one of his rare breathtaking smiles. "You jealous?"

"Nope, just don't want to hear about it. Would you like to hear some of my stories?"

He frowns.

Mer's grins and lifts her plate in his direction. "She got you there."

I walk away, not wanting to hear them, and join Jacob at the table.

He looks up. "Hey, how pissed is Owen?"

I wink and sit across the table from him. "Not at all."

He smiles and lets out a deep breath. "Thank goodness. I've been gearing up for an argument all day."

I take a sip of water. "All is fine. I appreciate you looking out for him."

Owen sits down beside me. "You're not going to wait for me?"

I wave my fork at him. "Nope, you were too busy arguing with your sister. I'm hungry. Priorities."

Owen chuckles. "All right, you made your point. Now, put your fork down and stop waving it around like a weapon."

Jacob has a more relaxed smirk on his face. "I like seeing you like this. She's really good for you."

"Yeah, I kinda like her being around, too." He leans over to kiss me on the cheek.

Will I ever get use to his public displays of affection?

Mer smiles. "Aww, you made her blush."

I stick my tongue out at her and just focus on eating, even though it seems like everyone's eyes are on me. Haven't they seen a girl blush before?

Owen's body is still shaking with laughter, and once again, I find myself reverting back to my old habit of wanting to disappear. I take a deep breath and steady myself.

The table is quiet for a few more minutes until Rose decides to join us. "Hey, baby. Finally come to your senses?"

She wraps her arms around Owen, and anger fills me. Before I can open my mouth, Owen disentangles himself from her. "Don't touch me, Rose."

"Are you serious?" she snarls.

He takes a deep breath and looks in her eyes. "Look, you were just a distraction. I'm sorry, but you obviously thought it was something more than it really was. I thought I had made that clear, but apparently I didn't."

She saunters back to him, playing with a strand of her hair. "Okay, so let me still be your escape, then."

I move to get up, ready to deal with her myself, but before I can, he's in my head. *This is my battle, so let me handle this, just like you'll need to handle your own.*

He better damn well hurry this up.

He pulls me up out of my seat and to his side. "Rose, I don't need a distraction anymore. Ariah is it for me."

Her face turns red and her voice comes out harsh. "A freaking outsider? Are you serious?"

The dining area is now quieting down, and the people sitting nearest to us are looking over.

Owen turns to me, his gaze soft. "Yes, I'm serious. She's

not going anywhere, so everyone better get used to her being around."

"If you think that, you're delusional. She is up to no good. When things between us were getting serious, she ran away to get your attention, and for some reason, it worked. She's manipulating you," Rose sneers.

Okay, I hate her as much as Elizabeth. I really want to punch her, but I bite my tongue.

Owen stands up and his tone has now turned commanding. "No, she isn't. We are connected in a way no one can understand but the two of us. I was using you to keep my distance from her. I hurt her, and she ran away because of it. That was on me, but it won't happen again. Now, I've put up with your disrespect long enough. Remember who your king is? If you can't, I will remind you."

This is the Owen I met when I first got here. The one that is in full control and will not tolerate any disobedience. Despite his outward demeanor, he has his thumb caressing my side. For some reason, this brings me comfort.

Rose narrows her eyes and looks at me. She walks past me. "Watch your back."

I'm about to go after her, but Owen holds me in place. He pulls me closer to his side and quickly kisses my lips.

Mer looks at me from the corner of her eye. "Wow. I've always known she was unbalanced, but now we definitely know she's psycho."

Owen shakes his head in disgust. "Ugh, why was I so stupid?"

I glance up at him. "Yeah, why were you?"

Jacob laughs.

Owen rubs a hand down his face. "I have no clue. I'm so sorry, princess."

Mer shrugs. "Well, at least you woke up. It's just sad that it took you this long. Rose only liked you for your title anyway."

I don't want to hear this, even if it's people saying negative things about her. "All right, I've had enough fun for the evening. I'm heading home."

I make my way to the door, before anyone can stop me.

As soon as I take a step outside, Owen is beside me and taking my hand. "I hate that you're hurting."

Does he really think that's it? "Owen, yes, I don't like to think about you two together, but it's more than that. I'm tired of being bullied. You didn't want me to step in, because you strung her along, which I hate, but it's more than that. All my life, I've been put down and beaten. It ends now."

We've reached the door to my house, and he quickly unlocks it with his key. "Really, you carry around the key to my home, too?"

He gives me a flirtatious smile. "Well, yeah. I need to be able to get to you."

I shake my head and giggle. He walks over to me and puts his hand on the side of my face. He leans in and briefly kisses me but quickly pulls back.

What does he think he's doing? "Hey."

"We aren't done talking. What do you mean, you've always been put down and beaten?"

I sigh, not really wanting to talk about this, but I did bring it up. "King Percy and Princess Elizabeth of Agrolon. The king liked to belittle and beat my brother and me, while the princess was just plain cruel."

Owen stills. "Wait, the king beat you?"

"Yes. My brother and I were beaten a lot as kids, but we

learned quickly how to keep hidden. However, Elizabeth liked to do things and blame us."

His eyes turn angry. "What did your mother and father say?"

"Father and Emerson, my sister, stayed on the king's side of the palace. As soon as the prophesized Savior was born, they were to stay near the king. My father knew of the beatings, but he just didn't seem to care." I close my eyes, not wanting to see the expression on his face. Why am I telling him this? What if he changes his mind? I sit down on the couch and tap my foot.

He stays put, but is watching my every move. "What about your mother?"

"Well, she wasn't aware of the beatings but knew that the royal family wasn't fond of us. The only exception was Nick."

He tenses at my words. "Were you close? I mean, you called the king and princess by their titles or full name, but yet, you're calling Prince Nickolas by a nickname?"

I take a deep breath. Why did I let that slip? "Yes, I told you earlier that we were close. He was one of the few people who was nice to me, especially growing up."

He closes his eyes and is silent for a moment. He finally asks softly. "How close?"

"Well, as kids, we were best friends. When we got older..." I trail off, not really wanting to go there again.

"You really had a relationship with the prince of Agrolon, and the prince of Orlon gave you an engagement ring?"

This sounds so bad. I cringe. "Yes, but Nick is now married to my sister, and Sam was going to ask for the ring back."

He comes toward me and sits down on the table directly

in front of me. His eyes search mine. "So, what does that mean? Am I just convenient?"

Wait, what's going on? Why would he think that? "Are you crazy? Do you think you're convenient? You were a jerk when I got here, so let's not forget that. Nick was my childhood crush who turned out to be a coward. I don't know what Sam was, but I started having doubts about him shortly after leaving Agrolon. After that first time I saw you, you were always on my mind, and I couldn't shake you. But I had no place to go, so I was trapped."

His face turns sinister, his jade green eyes unreadable. "So, is that why you're with me and here? Because you don't have a place to go?"

"Maybe at first. I won't lie. However, not now. I've always felt a pull to be here. I found your place on my way to Orlon. When I saw you, you took my breath away. I couldn't get you out of my mind. I dreamed about you. Now, after being here and getting to know you, everything has changed," my words get shaky.

"Changed how? You feel something for me?" He shifts where he is sitting beside me and leans into me. His chest is pressing against mine.

I push against his chest. "Why are you acting this way? I get to see Rose hang all over you, but you get upset just from hearing about my past? That's not fair."

His eyes spark, and he moves my hands away. "No one ever asked me to marry them. Do you know what it was like, seeing you in a royal dress? I didn't even know you, but I felt like my heart was ripped out. I have never had feelings like this for anyone, let alone some headstrong, beautiful woman that just stumbled her way into our hidden lands. You scared the hell out of me, and now you're mine."

He dips his head and roughly kisses me. He's gently biting and deepening our kiss. I match his intensity, and our powers collide into one another. It isn't like earlier; this is all-encompassing, and between the power thrumming through us and our mouths together, we both surrender ourselves completely to one another.

Chapter Twenty

I wake up cocooned in Owen's arms, my back against his chest. My eyes pop open, and the night before pours into my mind. Last night was amazing, and there is no turning back at this point. Not that I wanted to, anyway, but the thought of being invested in someone again terrifies me.

After last night, everything is clear now. Nick was just a crush, and Sam... He was just a good friend. How did I not realize that until just now? Owen is it for me.

He glides his fingertips up my arm and chuckles. "Is your brain already working overtime?"

I flip over to face him, and he grins at me, then kisses my lips. "Good morning, princess."

"I'm stuck with that nickname, aren't I?"

He pecks the tip of my nose. "Yep."

I sigh, and he laughs.

He traces my lips with his fingers and his tone is very tender. "Last night officially changed everything. You know that, right?"

I lick my lips. "Yes, I know. Do you regret it?"

He grins and traces my tattoo. "No, princess. In fact, I wish I hadn't fought what was between us for as long as I did. You're mine in every way now, and nothing is going to change that."

For once in my life, I believe him with no doubts. The last shred of my hesitance falls to the wayside. I giggle. "I'm okay with that."

He kisses me once again and pulls back, looking me in the eye. "Ariah, I love you."

My heart quickens in pace, and I'm sure I have a stupid looking grin on my face. "I love you, too."

"Well, then, I guess I should officially ask you to be my date for tonight's party."

I arch an eyebrow. "Okay, maybe you should do that?"

He grunts and tickles my ribs. I squeal, and he is over me, pinning me down within seconds. I could get him off me if I really wanted to, but why would I? "Will you please give me the honor of escorting you to the party?"

I try to hide my grin, but it's pointless. I've never been this happy before. "Hmmm... I'll have to think about it. After all, the first time, you told me I was going with you."

He widens his eyes in fake shock and tickles me again.

I laugh until tears are falling down my face, and I try to squirm away.

His grip is unrelenting. "Oh, no you don't. Not until you say yes."

"Yes, Yes. Please stop tickling me!"

He dips is head down, resting his forehead against mine. "See, I get what I want." He then gives me another kiss.

We get lost in our own little world, and things are getting heated when there is a loud knock on my bedroom door.

Oh, no. Please don't let it be her.

The doorknob starts turning, and I'm so happy that I locked that door.

Mer's voice makes me cringe. "Ariah, come on. Let me in. You know that you really don't mind me just barging in."

I try to crawl out of bed to find a place for him to hide, but he holds me down. He winks at me and I'm shaking my head. Oh, dear goodness, please just be quiet.

He gives me an evil grin. "Mer, there may be a reason the door is locked."

My mouth drops open. Did he really just do that?

There is silence on the other side of the door for a few seconds before there is a loud "Eewwwww."

Within seconds, my front door shuts, letting me know she must have left. "Owen, oh my goodness. Why'd you do that?"

"Ariah, things have been changing, but as of today, you're mine in every way. Everyone will know, and my kingdom will accept you. We are bonded, and there is no reason for you to be embarrassed. You know our bond is more sacred than a marriage, right?"

When he puts it that way, how can I argue? "Well, yes, I guess, but I hadn't thought of it like that. Okay, you're right. I'm in." I look him in the eye, wanting him to know I am serious.

He smiles and kisses my lips again. "As much as I'd like to stay here with you all day, Mother did say we both need to train today. Let's go get something to eat before she sends Mer back to us again."

I exhale and get up from the bed. I take a quick shower, and by the time I walk out, Owen is dressed and is waiting for me. Within minutes, I have my clean black outfit on and my hair in a ponytail. I glance at him as I head toward the door. "You ready?"

He grins and gets up following me down the stairs. "I'm waiting on you."

I head out the door and turn around, walking backwards. "Well, look at who is out the door first." I stick my tongue out at him.

He laughs and takes my hand, leading us to the food. We walk into the dining hall and each of us grab a plate. After we fill them up, we join Mer and Jacob at the table.

Mer smirks. "So… how was your morning?"

Of course, she would go there. Why can't some things just not be addressed?

However, Owen meets her head on. "Best morning ever. In fact, there will be many mornings like that from here on."

Jacob takes a break from eating. "Oh, really? What happened? Did I miss something?" He glances at me with concern. "Ariah, why is your face so red?"

Mer waggles her eyebrows. "Well, it seems like they are officially *together*, if you know what I mean."

Oh, my goodness. Could this get any more uncomfortable? I look at my food, completely averting my eyes from everyone at the table.

Jacobs looks at Owen and then me. "Wait…"

Owen wraps his arm around me and pulls me closer into his side. "Yes, we are officially together. I mean, we were yesterday, too, but we've completed the bond now."

Owen tilts my head up, so he can kiss me. He then looks at Mer. "Quit trying to make Ariah feel uncomfortable. You've had your fun."

Jacob is perplexed. "Wait… what bond? And how does Mer know this?"

Owen winks at me. "We're soulmates."

Jacob's jaw drops and his eyes are wide. "Are you serious?"

This is all Mer's fault. This whole uncomfortable conversation. I point my finger at her. "Yes, and she has boundary issues. I keep telling you all this."

"Don't worry. I've learned my lesson after this morning." She gags.

I cross my arms. "Good. I would have done that a whole lot sooner if that's all it took."

Owen raises an eyebrow. "Is that so?"

"Maybe…" I wink.

He grins and leans over to kiss me my lips again.

"And I thought they were bad before," Mer grumbles.

Jacob pushes his plate aside. "How do you know you're soulmates?"

"Look." Owen grabs my wrist and turns it over so his is right next to mine. Our tattoos are front, center and identical.

Jacob just stares and looks at them in awe. "I always thought that was just for the Originals."

Owen nods. "Me, too. But these appeared after the first time Ariah and I used our powers together."

Jacob glances up at us. "I'm not surprised. You always seemed to be drawn to one another, despite both of you fighting it. It was almost supernatural."

I glance outside and realize that we're running late. "Owen, we have to go. Your mother is probably wondering where we are."

His gaze follows mine. "You're right. Let's go. Are we all going to the party together?"

"Oh, of course, we are. Ariah and I are getting ready

together. You and Jacob can pick us up like nice boys," Mer answers.

Huh, that's a new fact. "Oh, you guys are going together?"

"Yes, we go together every year. That way we can actually have fun instead of worrying about a real date," she answers.

As soon as she says that, Jacob flinches. That's interesting. Not wanting to be late, I move toward the door. Owen is beside me within seconds.

We rush across the village and get to the training area within minutes.

Willow is leaning against a tree. "It's about time you two decided to show up."

"Sorry, Mother. We just lost track of time."

I'm burning up from our hurry to get here, so I take my jacket off, trying to cool down. As soon as I drop it on the ground, Willow's eyes are on me.

She walks over to me and touches my upper arm. "You completed the bond."

How does she know this? I'm giving up on any kind of privacy whatsoever. I'm speechless and not sure what to say.

Owen's forehead creases. "Yes, we did. We didn't mean for it to happen. It just kind of did."

Even though his words are true, they hurt me all the same. Does he regret it? Would he rather us have waited or never completed the bond?

His eyes soften. *"Don't be silly, princess. I'd have done it earlier if you'd have given me a chance. There was no getting rid of me before, and you definitely can't now. We are each other's in every way."*

His gaze goes back to his mother. "How did you know?"

She points to my upper arm. "Look."

My breath catches in my chest. Now, on my arm is the

exact same tattoo that's found on my wrist. However, it's a bigger version, and the thorns run down my arm, connecting to the tattoo on my wrist.

I glance up. "Owen, do you have one?"

He takes his jacket off, and, of course, he has the exact same one on him.

"That's how I knew," she answers.

Willow smiles at us. "We need to practice." She walks over and pats me softly on the cheek. "And, sweet girl, welcome to the family."

So, for the next several hours, Owen and I work together and by ourselves, strengthening our power.

۞

The most amazing thing is that, even though we practiced for hours, I am not drained at all. Willow explained it's because we are actually rejuvenating each other. That's one of many benefits of a bonded relationship.

Willow releases us, because she's drained, and we all need to get ready for the big celebration tonight. Apparently, it is a bigger deal than I realized. This celebration is one done to honor the current and prior kings of Noslon. It's been a tradition for hundreds of years.

Much to my horror, Mer is in my house, setting up. The nude-colored dress I had picked out is hanging in the living room, and a table with all kinds of make-up is set up in my bathroom.

Mer steps out and is already made up. "Hey, perfect timing. I figured we'd just get ready here. I just finished my makeup and hair, so I'm ready to start on you."

She looks gorgeous. She has brown eyeshadow on, which makes her eyes pop, and she's wearing a dark pink lipstick. Her hair is pulled into an elegant up-do that highlights her neck.

I go sit in the chair positioned next to the make-up. She grins and goes to town. Surprisingly, she's not talkative like my mother, and I find that I'm enjoying it. Within a few minutes, she's working on my hair.

She leans back and tilts her head. "You're all done. Want to take a look?"

I grin. "Yes. I'm dying to see."

I get up and look in the mirror. It takes me a minute to realize that I'm looking at me. I have dark charcoal around my eyes that emphasizes their gray color. My lips are a dark red, and my hair is in loose curls, cascading down my shoulders. But what really makes the difference is that, for the first time ever, I look happy. "You work magic, Mer."

Mer snorts. "Girl, you look amazing naturally. Most of it is just you."

I grab my dress and walk into my bedroom to change. When I walk back out, Mer is sitting on the couch, tapping her foot.

She glances at me. "Ariah, we didn't get off on the right foot. I honestly thought you were just trying to use us or take advantage of Owen at first. But, after a few weeks, when you kept to yourself and didn't ask for anything, well, I knew I had misjudged you."

I'm not sure where this is going. How do I respond to that?

Mer laughs. "I guess, what I'm trying to say is that I'd like for us to be friends. I mean, I think we are now, but I just wanted to get it out there. You're now my sister in every way, and well, I've got your back."

"Mer, we're good. Honestly, I took your words at our very first meeting to heart. I think it helped me with several instances between then and now. I guess, what I'm saying is, don't worry about it. We're family now."

She gives me the biggest smile I've ever seen from her. "Look, Owen's been on me, saying I need to tell you this and he's right. We're family now. Even though I don't have powers like you and Owen, I do have a special ability."

My eyes widen.

Mer bites her lip and takes a deep breath. "I can tell how powerful each person is and their intent."

"Really? How long have you been able to do this?" This is intriguing. Lydia can see the intent of one's power as well.

She opens her mouth to say more, but there is a loud knock at my door, followed by it opening.

Owen walks in and stops dead in his tracks once he sees me. "You're absolutely breathtaking."

I grin, scanning him from head to toe. "You're pretty good-looking yourself."

He has his standard black on, but his outfit is more on the dressy side. He has a crown on his head, but it looks more rugged than elegant. This is a man that can get things done and is worth trusting.

Jacob walks in. "Okay, now I see what Mer is getting at. You guys are getting disgustingly sweet." His attention shifts to the other woman in the room. "Mer, you look lovely, as well."

Within minutes, we're all walking toward the dining hall that has been converted into a dance floor. Everyone stops and bows when Owen walks in. However, Rose comes over and cuts me off so that we get separated.

"You don't belong up there with him," she hisses.

Owen continues through the room and up to a throne area the villagers created. He sits down in the only chair up there and looks around. His eyes land directly on me. "Tonight, we celebrate the royal family and all the forefathers that helped bring us to our current state. Without their guidance, we would have struggled to survive. Let us remember that, if given a chance, people can do incredible things. On that note, Jacob, can you please bring another chair up here next to mine."

Murmurs are heard everywhere while Mer is grinning wide. Jacob pauses for a minute but quickly pulls himself together, walking into the next room and bringing out another chair just like Owen's. As he sets it down next to Owen, I turn around and find Willow in the back of the room.

Owen's eyes find mine again. "Ariah, will you please join me?"

The murmurs stop, and there is complete silence in the room. I slowly make my way to Owen, and he meets me right before the chairs. What in Knova is going on?

"I hope you're ready for this."

What does he mean 'ready for this'? *"What are you talking about?"*

"As I mentioned yesterday, Ariah is it for me. It's time for everyone to realize that she's now one of us and not going anywhere." He glances at me and takes my hand. I'm surprised to find him trembling. What am I missing?

He drops down on one knee in front of everyone. My

heart sputters to life. He can't be doing what it looks like, right?

He looks up at me. "Ariah, you've been a pain in my ass since the first day I saw you. I was determined to keep my distance from you, because you were an unknown. Thankfully, you made sure that didn't happen. You challenge me in a way nobody ever has. You make me feel things that I never thought I'd want to. I'm so glad you broke down my walls, and I always want you by my side. What I'm getting at not so eloquently is… Ariah, will you marry me?"

The breath is knocked out of me, and there are no reservations about my answer. I bob my head yes, unable to speak. The whole room disappears, and he smiles at my answer.

Mer walks over to him and puts something in his hand. I soon realize that it's a ring, and he quickly slips it on my left ring finger. It's a very simple ring, but it's beautiful in its own right. It's a single gold band that looks like thorns wrapping around my finger with a black stone in the center. It's identical to the thorns on the key and our tattoos.

As soon as it's on my finger, it feels like a part of me has been found. Owen quickly stands and kisses me in front of everyone. After a few seconds, the crowd applauds, and there are whistles thrown our way. Embarrassed by the attention, I pull back. He smiles, touching his forehead to mine. "Thank goodness, you said yes. I didn't know how you'd react."

I giggle. "Is that why you were trembling?"

He reaches down and touches the ring on my finger. "You have no idea how vulnerable I just was. I've never been scared like that." He lifts my hand and places it on his heart. His tone soft and gentle. "I'd do anything for you."

Love like never before fills me. For once, there is no question if we're meant to be together. Even if we didn't have matching tattoos, I would still know that he is mine.

His lips find mine once more, and then he takes me to my throne next to his. As soon as I settle, Rose rushes across the room and out the door. One less thing I have to deal with tonight. I focus back on the people who are dressed up nice for a night of fun. The music starts, and couples begin dancing.

After a short while, Owen takes my hand. "Would you like to dance, princess?"

"Yes, I really would."

He smiles and pulls me to my feet. "Come on, let's show them how it's done."

I giggle in response and follow him onto the floor. He's actually an excellent dancer, and for once, I'm able to truly enjoy myself. A few songs later, Mer and Jacob join us. We all have fun and mingle with everyone.

After a while, I need something to drink. I head off the dance floor when Mer catches up to me. "Hey, sis, I think I'll join you."

"Ha, we aren't married yet."

"Princess, if you really think that then we have a problem. One, your bond is stronger than marriage vows. You're more committed already than a wedding will ever make you. And, two, if Owen heard you say that, you'd be married tonight." She counts off on her fingers.

I laugh. She's right about that. I grab a drink from the table when the woman behind the table stops me.

She hands me a bubbling beverage. "Oh, we have something special for our future queen. Please, drink this."

I'm not a fan of alcohol, but I don't want to be rude and

insult her. So, I take a big sip, drinking over half. I cringe, and Mer bursts out laughing. "Not a big drinker, huh?"

I shake my head and notice that Owen is searching for me. I hurry back to him.

He pulls me close to him. "Where did you run off to? I don't want you going too far away without me. Half our people will accept you now that we're engaged, but the other half is livid. Don't go anywhere without me again."

Mer groans. "Oh, calm down. She was with me."

"I don't care. It doesn't happen again."

My vision grows foggy, and dizziness takes over.

Owen's focus is back on me. "Ariah, what's wrong?"

I lean against him, unable to stand on my own.

Mer snickers. "Oh, my goodness, she's such a lightweight."

Owen appears alarmed. "What are you talking about?"

She waves her hand. "Oh, Diane just gave her some spirits. She'll be fine in a little while."

"Mer, she isn't acting drunk."

I try to tell him not to worry, but find that I can't speak. What in the hell is going on?

Owen is frantic and wraps his arms around my waist. "Ariah, talk to me."

I try again with no luck.

He tightens his grip around me. "Talk to me through our bond."

Oh, yeah. I guess I could try that. *"Owen, I feel off. I'm dizzy, and my vision is getting blurrier by the second."*

He scoops me up in his arms and heads for the door.

Willow is standing there, waiting for us. "Bring her to my house, now."

Owen nods, and we quickly leave the party and make it to

the house. Once we are inside, I can barely make anything out. My vision is mostly gone.

He gently lays me on the couch. "Mother, what's wrong?"

"Someone must have poisoned her. I'm not surprised. I found a bush of death berries that looked like someone had picked."

He faces turns pale white. "What? No, there has to be something we can do. That I can do."

Willow exhales loudly. "Calm down and let me focus, boy."

She moves around and gathers some items.

My power is going crazy inside, and it appears to be trying to fight back. My vision goes black. So, this is how I die?

Owen rests his forehead on mine. "It's going to be okay, baby. We'll find a way." He repeats those words over and over.

I feel tears running down my face, and I'm unsure if they are mine or his.

Willow shuffles back over to me. "Owen, move. Hurry, it's taking a toll, and her power is fighting back."

She rubs something cool on my arms and legs. She's whispering as she does it, but I can't make out her words.

After a few minutes, she caresses my cheek. "I know you can heal. I've seen it in my visions. Focus your power on healing your body and not trying to attack it. That's the only way you're going to make it out of this alive."

Why hadn't I thought of that? Unlike when I healed Pierce, I pour my power inside of me instead of out. I pull from the elements surrounding me and try to focus them all inward.

Willow reaches out and grabs Owen's hand. "Owen,

connect with her. You are one, and you'll be able to give her strength."

Within seconds, Owen's there, and I feel his power merging with mine. We stay like that for a while, and eventually, I'm not as dizzy. I open my eyes and find that my vision has returned. I still focus for a few more minutes, wanting to make sure whatever was in me is gone.

I tap Owen's hands, and he quickly opens his eyes. "Are you okay?"

I attempt to smile. "Well, I'm tired, but we did use a lot of power, and someone did just try to kill me. However, I think I'll make a full recovery."

He glares at me. Of course, he doesn't find it funny.

He gathers me into his arms. "Let's get you home."

Willow comes over and pats my arm. She sternly glances at Owen. "She does need rest, so don't do anything crazy tonight. You can deal with the problem tomorrow. Make them sweat it out."

Owen nods his head, and then walks us out the door. His mother only lives a few houses down, so we are home within minutes.

Owen takes me upstairs and lays me on the bed.

I curl up in a ball. "Go on home. I can get dressed. I know you have to be tired."

He turns an angry face toward me. "Don't you even think about it. First off, I am home. I'd have you move in with me, but for some reason, this feels like where we are meant to live. Secondly, I'm taking care of you, so lie down and let me handle this."

He leaves the room and returns with some nice-looking pajamas.

I perk up. "Hey, where'd you get those?"

"Mer gave them to me for you. She said that you are to throw those awful handmade ones away."

I snort, because that's what attractive ladies do.

He shakes his head and moves over to remove my dress.

I pull the covers over me. "Hey, I can get myself dressed. I'll let you know when you can come back in."

"You do realize I've seen what's under there. Stop being ridiculous," he chastises, removing the covers and helping me change.

Honestly, I'm still really weak, so it's nice to have the help.

When I'm all settled, he slips into his night clothes and crawls into bed right beside me. He tugs me into his arms, and I nestle against his chest.

He kisses my forehead. "Sleep well, my love. Tomorrow, we have some business to take care of."

For some reason, I kind of feel sorry for Diane. With that odd thought, I fall right to sleep.

Chapter Twenty-One

I wake up, cuddling with the most handsome guy in the world. It makes me so happy that he stayed to watch over me. I watch him sleep. Times likes this it's hard to imagine he's already a king.

He opens his eyes. "That's getting kind of creepy."

How did he know? I can't believe he caught me.

He laughs. "Morning, beautiful." He leans up kissing my lips. "How are you feeling?"

"Actually, I feel like my normal self this morning. Whatever we did last night took care of the problem."

He narrows his eyes. "Diane will pay for this today."

I arch an eyebrow. "Hey, did you forget? I think your exact words were 'This is my battle so let me handle this, just like you'll need to handle your own.'"

He sits up. "No one tried to kill me."

I tilt my head. "Still, there was no disclaimer when you said that."

He lets out a deep breath. "Ariah, you're going to be the death of me."

I giggle and kiss him again. He resists at first, but finally caves, giving into me. We spend the next little while enjoying each other's company.

❧

We drag ourselves over to breakfast. As soon as we walk in the door, Mer gets up from the table and runs over to give me a huge hug. "Oh, my goodness, Ari, are you okay?"

Owen grabs her arm, roughly pulling her away from me. "You don't get to be comforted. You should have known that something like that was going to happen."

Her eyes widen. "Are you seriously trying to blame me? It was Diane. How was I to know?"

The people at the buffet line turn toward us, watching the scene unfold.

This is not good. I walk over and put my hand on Owen's shoulder. "Hey, calm down, please. Can we go outside? We're causing a scene."

He relaxes under my touch and nods, then takes my hand and leads me out the door, with Mer and Jacob following close behind.

Before anyone else can say anything, I speak up. "Owen, don't be mean to your sister. It's not her fault. We were having a good time and celebrating our engagement. We didn't consider there would be any danger, and you can't fault her for that."

He groans and rubs his free hand down his face. "You're right. I'm sorry, but I felt so helpless. You could have died last night. I'm so mad at myself for not protecting you. I'm sorry I took it out on you, Mer."

Mer and Jacob stand there with astonished expressions on their faces.

"Um… it's okay. I'm just glad she's okay."

My heart warms at his declaration. "You can't always protect me. I've learned that I have to be able to stand on my own. You can't always be around."

He turns toward me and grab my hands, wrapping them around him. "Why do you have to be so logical? I'm thinking I just need to chain you to me."

Jacob groans. "Okay, as much fun as this is to watch, how are we going to handle Diane?"

Owen lets my arms go. "We're going to eat breakfast, because Ariah needs her strength after last night. Then, we will go to the fields for an impromptu meeting."

I'm all good with eating. I'm famished, and food sounds really good right about now.

We all walk back into the dining hall, and Mer and Jacob walk back to the table they had been sitting at. Luckily, their food is still there.

Owen and I gather our breakfast and join them at the table.

I feel as if everywhere we go people are staring. "Wow, people really watch you all when you argue."

Jacob takes a huge bite of food. "Well, they were also surprised to see you alive. When we walked in this morning, the rumor had circulated that you were dead."

Mer flinches. "What is wrong with you? It's not normal to say something like that with no emotion."

His forehead creases. "Am I supposed to be weeping or something?"

"A little emotion would be good." Mer points to his face. "Maybe act like you would care if she died."

I shake my head, needing her to calm down. "We have enough drama, Mer. How he said it was fine."

Owen just grins and keeps eating, not saying a word.

There is a little bit of tension in the air. I'm assuming it's because everyone is focused on what's going to happen next.

We all finish and get up to leave. We head to the fields, because, apparently, Diane works in the herbal area that is used in the medicines.

Everyone we pass stares at me in awe. Yeah, I defied death again. How many more times is someone going to attempt to kill me?

Owen's head snaps in my direction. *"How many people have tried killing you, Ariah?"*

"Get out of my head, Owen."

Mer's eyes shine brightly. "What? You guys can mind-speak?"

We are now walking on the field, and Owen glares in my direction, completely ignoring Mer. "We will talk about this later."

I roll my eyes, and he snarls.

Someone walks up but stays several feet away, obviously alarmed that we are here. "Hey, Ariah, something I can help you with?"

I realize that Smiley has walked up to us. "Hey. How are you?"

He glances around at everyone, then looks down at his fingers. "Uh… fine, but I'm wondering what I can help you all with."

Owen steps in between the two of us, and Smiley shifts even more.

I attempt to walk around Owen, and he reaches out,

pulling me toward him, resting his arm around my waist. I glare up at him. *"Seriously? You know I'm yours."*

Owen cuts his eyes down to me. *"Just want to make sure he understands that you're mine now."*

I snort, and Smiley has begun tapping his foot.

We must look crazy just standing here, staring at one another. *"I think everyone knows we are engaged. We're good."*

Owen scowls at Steve. "Where's Diane?"

He glances up from his finger. "Diane?"

Owen stiffens, his tone short. "Yes, did I stutter?"

I want to say something to Owen. He's being mean, but right now, he's barely keeping it together.

Smiley shakes his head. "No. No, sir. Here, I'll take you to her." He walks us deeper into the fields.

As we pass people working, they try to make it seem like they are not watching us.

Yes, I'm alive, and we are here. I almost feel like I'm part of a circus.

When we approach a large circle of women, Diane looks up, and her face pales.

Owen glares at her, his tone steel. "Diane, you need to come with us."

She takes a step back. "Oh, sir, I can't right now. I'm helping these ladies pick their daily allotments. I don't want them to get into trouble."

"They'll be pardoned today. You will join us."

Diane stays frozen in place, not even attempting to move. The group around her is silent.

Mer and Jacob have followed behind us, and I've completely forgotten that they are there until Jacob steps up.

"Your king has requested your presence. If you don't move, I'll make you." Jacob looks fierce right now, similar to the first day I met him. His blue eyes are hard, and his muscular body is tight, almost as if it's ready to attack.

This has her moving and joining our group.

Jacob falls into step behind her as we make our way back to the village center.

We enter Owen's house, and he motions for her to sit on the couch.

She's fidgeting and jerking around, obviously guilty and not wanting to be here. "Why did you try to kill Ariah?" Owen bursts out.

His bluntness catches her off guard. She quivers. "I didn't know what exactly was in the drink. Someone gave it to me and said it was for Ariah. I didn't realize until I saw how she was acting that it was poison."

He hovers over her, shaking with rage. "What the hell is wrong with you?"

Diane is crying now, and Owen is on edge.

I sit down beside her and try to keep my voice calm. "Who gave you the poison?"

She cries harder and tries to talk, but she's a blubbering mess.

I reach over and squeeze her hand. "It's okay. Calm down, but you know we need to understand who all was involved."

She takes deep breaths and wipes the tears from her cheeks. "It was Rose. She said that an outsider isn't fit to be queen and that the drink would show how weak and pathetic you are. Owen wouldn't want to be with you then, and she would be queen and pardon my involvement."

Owen exhales and softly speaks. "Go get Rose right now, Jacob. We will meet you in the town square."

He glances at Mer. "Go ring the bell. There's a mandatory meeting that I want every single villager attending."

Jacob runs out of the room.

Mer's eyes widen. "Owen, we haven't rung that bell in years…"

His composure is about to snap. "I said do it *now*!"

Mer nods and quickly leaves the house.

Diane begins sobbing once again.

Owen cuts his eyes to her. "Come on, Diane. We're heading to the town square right now."

She nods and follows us.

The bell rings, and it's so loud that my insides vibrate.

Within minutes, people are rushing to the village center, wondering what's going on.

Willow appears, but stands in the back, off to the side, taking everything in.

Soon, the place is packed, and Owen, Diane, and I are on a platform.

Jacob must be close, because screams and pleas echo through the air.

A few moments later, Jacob appears carrying a fighting Rose. He hurries and stands on the platform next to us, depositing Rose right next to Diane.

When Rose sees me, her eyes widen. "Impossible."

Owen's face is rigid. "Why is that, Rose?"

Rose points at me. "She should be dead! I am supposed to be queen."

Before Owen can do anything crazy, I step toward her. "What did I ever do to you?"

She spits at me. "Do you really think this is about something you've done? You're an outsider and don't deserve to have him. No one here will ever accept you as one of us."

Owen turns to the crowd. "Is that true?"

The crowd remains quiet, not providing an answer.

Owen's face turns to one of disgust. "Well, whether you like it or not, *she* is one of us. Everyone is aware that we're engaged. However, you don't know the extent of our relationship."

He walks over to me and looks directly into my eyes. *"Please, remove your jacket."*

Deciding to trust him, I do what he asks. The cool air whips around me, and soon, he's removed his jacket as well.

He looks back out at the crowd. "We are bonded. We're soulmates. If this doesn't prove that she was meant to be one of us, I don't know what else will." He moves next to me, showing our matching tattoos that have taken on an ethereal tone.

I hear a few gasps.

Rose cries out, "That's not possible."

Diane breaks down and apologizes over and over again.

The women that were in the medicinal gardens with Diane are all speaking to each at once, while most of the others are stunned.

Owen takes a deep breath and watches the whole scene. "So, now, you all know that she is already your queen. The punishment for harming one of us is death. However, since the act was against Ariah, I'll let my mate make the call on punishment."

What? He's letting me make the decision? I've never led before. How am I to know what to do?

Everyone is watching me, and I realize I have to do something.

Owen steps back, allowing me to have the stage to myself.

I take a deep breath and turn to look at Rose and Diane.

Rose is glaring at me with hatred while Diane is still sobbing.

"Rose, you're banished from here. This is no longer your home. These are no longer your people, and if anyone has a problem with it, they can leave with you."

Rose glares at me with pure hatred. "You…" But before she can finish her sentence, Owen is there in a flash.

His tone drips with disdain. "You better not say a word. If it were up to me, you'd already be dead. Be grateful that the queen is so merciful."

She stumbles back, desperation on her face.

Ignoring her at this point, I turn to Diane.

She looks at me, quivering, and walks over to me, falling at my feet. "I'm so sorry. I should never have given you the drink, but I thought Rose was right. We will both leave right now."

How can I let someone so remorseful have such a harsh punishment? Her only crime was trusting Rose. Being exiled is too harsh for that.

Diane rises to her feet and shuffles toward the end of the platform.

I take a deep breath, steadying my next words. "Diane, you are forgiven. However, you will help out in the kitchen after your shift in the fields is over for the next year. That will be your punishment."

Diane turns to me with surprise clearly on her face. "You're not banishing me?"

"No, but if you ever willfully make a decision that puts any of us in danger like that again, you will be banished from the kingdom forever, the same punishment as Rose. I believe in second chances in certain situations, but you will not get a third. Do you understand?"

She nods and bows to me. "Thank you so much. I will make this up to you."

Did she really just bow to me? She doesn't need to do that.

"Jacob, show Rose to the forest." Owen takes his place beside me taking my hand and focusing on the crowd. "If anyone ever sees her attempting to return, let me know immediately. We will update the barrier, so she can't get back in. Diane, get back to the field. Your first shift in the kitchen will start today."

As we walk by Rose, she glares at me.

Willow plucks a piece of hair from her head, making Rose squeal, and heads to the lake.

Jacob comes over and grabs Rose, hauling her through the village toward the forest. She's screaming and yelling.

Maybe I made the wrong decision?

I'm about to call out to Jacob when Mer comes over and puts her hand on my shoulder. "Don't even think about it. If you let her come back, she'll do it again. She'll think you're weak."

Owen squeezes my hand, and I turn to face the crowd with him. "As you can see, my other half is kind and merciful, but do not forget that I am her other half. You all know how unforgiving I can be when my family is threatened. If anyone tries to harm her again, I will make the call on the punishment, and there will be no leniency. Is that clear?"

Half the crowd murmurs their understanding while the other half nod.

"Good, then let's get back to our business. Please, remember that there is still a group of people roaming our borders. Do not leave under any circumstances."

Some of the villagers immediately leave while the others stay and gossip.

Diane cautiously makes her way to me. "Thank you so

much, Your Highness. I've learned my lesson and am truly grateful for your forgiveness. Please, let me know if I can do anything at all for you." She walks off quickly, returning to the field.

Owen rubs my shoulder. "You okay?"

"Maybe I shouldn't have cast Rose out?"

"Princess, you should have done a lot more than that. What you did was kind and gracious. If it were up to me, her punishment would have been a lot worse," he reassures me.

Willow comes back to us. "It's been done. Rose cannot return. I wish you would have at least beat the snot out of that brat."

I laugh, and Owen kisses my forehead. "I think she did a wonderful job. Ariah is a natural-born leader."

Willow reaches out and gives me a hug. "I agree with you, but unfortunately, I don't think Rose will learn her lesson."

Jacob comes back, and he has scratch marks on his face.

Owen laughs. "She didn't go easily?"

"No, she did not. I think she may be tougher than most men my size," he grumbles.

Mer snorts. "Maybe you're just getting weak?"

He glares at her, but she just shrugs.

Owen looks at him. "Jacob, now that everyone knows about Ariah and me, I need to move some stuff. Can you help?"

He nods. "Absolutely. Let's go."

Within hours, Owen has all of his stuff moved into my, I mean, our house. We go to bed that night in each other's arms.

Chapter Twenty-Two

❦

A YEAR LATER

The sun shines through the window, waking me from a restless sleep.

"You okay, Ari?" Owen asks, half-asleep.

"Yeah, I didn't mean to wake you. Go back to sleep. I'm going to get some coffee."

I try to crawl out of bed, but he grabs my waist, pulling me beside him. "For the past week, you've had trouble sleeping. You aren't getting enough rest. Is everything okay?"

I smile sadly at him. "Yes, but for some reason, I keep dreaming of my brother. It seems as if he and Agrolon are in danger."

He kisses my lips. "I'm so sorry. I'm sure it's just your mind running wild."

"Well, your mother keeps saying that the West is getting ready to attack. Maybe they're about to?"

"Mother says a lot of things. Don't listen to her. She's just paranoid." He tucks a wayward strand of hair behind my ear.

I nod, but something seems off. I kiss his lips and wiggle out of his arms. I'm exhausted, and a hot cup of coffee is just what I need. Just as I sit down at the table, Owen joins me in the kitchen.

He glances out the window. "I think I'm going to go out and hunt today."

"But I thought we were still limiting the amount of time outside our borders. Aren't there still a lot of people roaming out there?"

He gives me a smile. "I know, baby. But we're running out of meat. We'll all grow weak without enough protein. I'll take Jacob with me, and we'll be very careful. I promise."

I roll my eyes and take a big sip. "You better be. I don't want to have to hunt you down or hurt you."

He chuckles and comes over, giving me one last peck. "I'll be home soon. I promise."

He walks out the door, and I'm left alone to my own thoughts. Normally, it doesn't bother me, but ever since my dreams have started, I need something to distract me.

There is a knock on my door, and Mer comes in with two big plates of food. "Owen said I should bring you food. So, lucky for you, I decided I wanted your company."

I shake my head and join her at the table. She's turned out to be a great sister and close friend since we decided to trust one another. Something about how I didn't act entitled and pulled my weight caused me to have favor in her eyes. Apparently, the day she told me about her special gift was the day I received her blessing.

When she finishes her food, she sets down her fork. "What are we doing today?"

"Well, I told Diane I'd help them in the fields."

She covers her face with her hands. "Ugh, why would you do that? What have I ever done to you?"

"Oh, stop. You don't have to help me. You can go sew or whatever else you do."

"You have gone from being an outsider to everyone's favorite little villager. So, yes, I will help. I need them to love me, too." She puts the back of her hand to her forehead.

I finish up, and we head out to the fields to help. We are picking some weeds that are used for herbs when I lose track of time. Before I realize it, it's getting dark. Where is Owen? He'd normally have come to find me by now.

I glance over at Mer. "We need to go."

"Oh, thank goodness. I thought you'd lost your damn mind with how long we've been out… Hey, what's wrong?" Her expression turns concerned when she looks at me.

"Owen, he should have come and found me by now."

"Why don't you talk to him? You've been bonded together for a year, and you always forget you can reach him whenever." She rolls her eyes.

I cringe. She's right. I always forget this. *Owen, where are you?*

After a few seconds, he responds. *"Princess, I'm so sorry. I'm here and was just about to come get you. We ran into some people, and we need to talk. Let's meet at the house."*

I take off.

Mer runs to catch up. "Hey, what's going on? Remember, I can't hear him."

I don't pause. "He said they ran into some people and that we need to talk. I'm meeting him at the cottage."

Within minutes, I'm through the door and find Willow, Owen, and Jacob at the table. "What's going on?"

Owen gets up and hugs me tight. His embrace is the best

thing in the world, and my worries are already calming. Knowing he's safe is all I needed. Everyone is quiet.

I look at him, and he frowns. "Your dreams might have actually been visions of your brother. The West is rising, getting ready to attack Agrolon and Orlon. Their next stop will be here."

"What? Well, Emerson will stop them. She's the Savior. This is her role."

Owen takes a deep breath, then lets it out. "Well, they still want us to rally. The Agrolon king believes that the power of three from the prophecy is referring to our three kingdoms coming together to fight the West."

My breath catches. "Wait... How do you know this?"

He grimaces. "The people outside our borders have been hunting for me. Under their king's order, they were instructed to find my father and request his presence at the palace. That falls to me since I'm now officially in charge. We ran into them today. We were chasing an animal in the woods and apparently didn't pay enough attention."

He should have never left. They should have stayed within the boarder. "What did you say?"

"What am I supposed to say?" He runs his hand down his face. "What if the king is right, and it's our countries that are supposed to come together?"

Is he crazy? "The Agrolon king won't be a good ruler for our country, either."

He rubs my arms. "Baby, he's not going to rule over us. Once it's done, I'll come back here to you."

"You think you're going without me?"

He slams his fist down on the table. "I don't want you back around that jackass."

I shake my head. "No, where you go, I go."

Willow stands. "We will all go."

Oh, crap. We aren't the only ones here. How'd I forget that?

Owen glares at his mother. "Why would we do that? I don't want Ariah anywhere near that asshole."

"Because it is time, and Ariah is right. The Agrolon king is corrupt and evil," Willow points to our wrists. "You are stronger together, and separating would not be wise. Also, you'll need back-up. The five of us will go."

Willow doesn't get like this often, and we've learned that, when she does, it's best if we listen. Am I really going back to Agrolon? They think I'm dead. However, I'd get to see Logan, Claire, and Mother. But that also comes with Nick, Elizabeth, and the king. Am I ready to see them?

Owen rubs calming circles on my back, which brings me some comfort. "I think we all need to sleep on this before we make any final decisions. It's getting late. Let's go eat, and we can meet back here in the morning. This isn't something that should be rushed."

Willow nods in agreement. "You're right. I'm going to go grab something and get home. There is a lot to think about."

She hugs us all and heads out.

Mer turns toward me when the door closes. "Come on, Ari. Let's go grab some food. You had me performing manual labor all day, and my tummy needs sustenance."

Owen looks at me confused. "Why were you performing manual labor?"

"Because she had to help Diane." Mer laughs.

Owen shakes his head. "You do remember she tried to kill you."

I wave my hand. "Ahh, she's made up for it. It's in the past."

"Ariah, it was just a year ago. You're too sweet for your own good. Don't worry, I'm here to protect you." He plucks me up in his arms.

I squeal, and Mer snorts.

Owen turns to Jacob. "Let's feed these women-folk before they faint from exertion."

Jacob smiles and follows us as we head to the dining hall.

"Owen, can you put me down now?"

He grins, looking down at me. "Not a chance. Today was the longest I've been away from you, and I need you next to me."

I wrap my arms around his neck. "I can walk next to you just fine."

He leans down to my ear. "But it's not nearly as fun."

Soon, we are all sitting at the table, eating our food and purposely avoiding the topic that's on everyone's mind.

"So, if we head to Agrolon, you do realize that your wedding will be postponed, right?" Mer pouts.

"Well, no, I hadn't thought that far. But if a war is coming, then it really isn't a good time for a wedding anyway." I tap my finger on the table.

Owen scowls at her. "Mer, drop it. We said we weren't going to talk about it until the morning. I'm tired anyway. You ready for bed, baby?"

I nod. I'm not hungry. We say our goodnights and walk back to our place hand-in-hand.

When we walk through the door, he turns me to face him "If you don't want to go, we won't."

I look around our place, our home. I don't want to leave here and go face my demons. "I don't want to go, but it's for very selfish reasons."

"As long as it's not because you still have feelings for those two princes, I'm good with it."

I look up at him in disbelief. How in Knova could he think that? My heart is all his. "Why would you say that?"

He looks down and kicks the ground. He's never acted like this, so I'm not sure what to do. "Well, I mean, that one was your first love, and then, the second rescued you after the king tried to murder you..."

"The first one was a friend that I grew up who that turned into something a little more. He was a coward. Sam wasn't love, just comfort. He wound up being a good friend. I just was confused about my feelings. You are the real deal for me. No one holds a candle compared to you. I love you with my entire being, and even our souls recognize each other," I turn his hand over so our matching tattoos stare at us.

"You're right. I just hate thinking of you with someone other than me," he grumbles.

"Hey, I had Rose staring me in my face." I glare at him.

"Okay, your point is made." He grins.

When we make it to the top of the stairs, I admit my fear. "I'll have to face my demons."

"Yes, if we go, you will. However, your kickass soulmate and fiancé will be there right next to you. If they come too close, I'll handicap them, so you can take them down."

I laugh, but that's one of the main differences between Owen and the other two. He will fight for me, protect me, but he also builds me up so I can stand by myself. He's not threatened by my abilities and encourages me to grow them.

Chapter Twenty-Three

W e both wake early, because the others will be arriving any minute. After our conversation last night, we both know that we can't risk the West taking over. They wouldn't just stop at Agrolon and Orlon. They would seek us out as well.

There is a knock at the door, and Owen opens it. Willow, Jacob, and Mer are all there together. Everyone is eager to make a decision. They walk in, and we all go into the living room. Mer, Willow, and I sit, while Owen and Jacob stand. I'm actually sitting between the other two ladies.

Owen looks at me. *So, we go?*

I nod. I guess we are doing this.

He looks at his mother. "All right, Ariah and I agree with Mother that we should go to Agrolon."

"When do we leave?" Jacob asks.

Owen looks out the window. "First thing tomorrow morning."

Looks like we aren't wasting any time. I take a deep

breath. "I guess we need to gather everything we'll need for the trip."

"I don't even know what to take. I've never been anywhere but here," Mer shrieks.

I tap the table with my finger. "You know those dresses we wore to the party, and all the others you have stashed away?"

Mer nods.

I glance at her. "Take every pretty dress you own. If you don't dress up, the king won't take you seriously. We need nice outfits for the men, as well. It's more about appearance than anything there. You play the role expected and dress the part. As long as you do that, you'll be fine."

Jacob gives me the same cruel grin I saw the first day I met him. It's been a while, and I forgot how much of a warrior he really is. "So, in other words, we aren't going to fit in."

I grin back. "Nope, we aren't. Good thing I gave up on that."

"Well, we can still at least look pretty." Mer eyes are lit with excitement. "I'm going to go gather all the stuff for that now."

She runs off to start on her chores.

Owen looks at Jacob. "Go make sure our carriages are still in order. It's been years since we used them, and they might need some maintenance. Goodness knows what all Mer is going to bring. We might need the whole fleet."

Jacob nods and leaves the house.

Willow walks over and touches my arm. "I will go gather the other things we will need, as well. This is truly the beginning of the war, and we all must be prepared."

She kisses both my and Owen's cheeks.

Within minutes, we are alone, just the two of us. "I'm going to go get Smiley to fill in while we are gone. Someone has to keep order. You going to be okay here by yourself?"

It makes me smile a little at his use of the nickname I had given Steve. I kiss his lips lightly. "Yes, go. I'll be fine. Make sure our village is taken care of, and I'll start packing our things."

He kisses my forehead and opens the door. "I won't be gone long."

As soon as I'm alone, I head to our bedroom to pack some of the things we will need. Mer will have most of the clothes we need to take, but not all of the necessities. Within a few days, I will get to see my brother again. My heart speeds up at that thought. How I've missed him. I can't wait until Owen meets my family and Claire.

Darkness tries to take over my thoughts, but I won't let it. I'm a different person now than I used to be. At my internal pep talk, my necklace warms. It hasn't done this since the day I found the box that can't be opened. I feel the familiar tug, and it guides me to the unopened box, of course. I guess this will be coming with us. As soon as I place it with our other things to pack, it returns to its normal temperature. Of course, it would start acting up again now.

After just a little while, I have everything we need packed and by the door. Owen comes back and looks around. "You're already done?"

"Yep, we're ready to go. Did you get everything taken care of in town?"

"Yes, Smiley is up for the job. I'm glad you talked me into giving him a chance. He really cares about our village and the people in it." He smiles at me.

I motion to the door. "Come on, let's go eat dinner. I'm

starving, and we need to check with Jacob about the carriages."

"Yes, ma'am." Owen salutes me.

I laugh, and we head out in search for Jacob. We find him at the barn on the edge of the village. He's all greased up and sweaty. Owen bends down, looking under the carriage. "How's it coming?"

Jacob stretches. "Fine, I just finished up the last one. You weren't kidding when you said they might need work. It's taken me all day, and I've gone nonstop."

Owen stands back up. "So, we can pack them down tonight?"

Jacob nods. "Do you doubt my abilities?"

I giggle. "No, never."

Owen grabs my hands and glances back at Jacob. "We're heading to eat. See you soon."

When we reach the dining hall, Mer is already there at our table. "Guys, I can't wait to show you what all I've made," she bounces.

Owen sighs. "Well, we'll have to see it when we get there. We need to get the carriages loaded down, so we can make it there as quickly as possible."

Mer deflates a little at that, but she soon gets excited again. We all quickly eat and leave to load everything up. It takes a little while to get everything together, but soon, we are all heading to our homes for a good night's rest.

۞

At dawn, we meet up at the carriages. I never thought I'd return to the palace, and I'm pretty sure I never really want to. As we head out, as soon as we are through the village's protective barrier, Ares appears.

I haven't seen him in ages, but he looks exactly the same. He comes over and walks beside the carriage.

Willow's eyes sparkle. "Oh, my goodness, is that the sacred stallion?"

I have no clue what they are talking about, but Owen is staring at Ares, too.

Mer points to my gray friend. "I told you all that I saw the horse with Ariah every time she was outside the boundary."

Owen watches me reach out and pet the stallion. "Yeah, I thought you were seeing things, that it was only the one day."

The carriage stops moving, and Jacob is yelling for Owen. He quickly gets out, and I'm right on his heels. He's not leaving me behind.

A man is dressed in Agrolon guardsman armor talking to Jacob.

Owen walks up to them. "What's going on?"

As soon as the guard turns, I can't believe my eyes.

He looks past Owen and stares right at me. Soon, he's moving toward me, completely ignoring Owen.

"Logan, is that really you?"

The End

About the Author

Jen L. Grey is a new, indie author who focuses on YA fantasy and paranormal genres.

Jen lives in Tennessee with her husband, two daughters, and toy Australian Shephard. Before she started writing, she was an avid reader and enjoyed being involved in the indie community. Her love for books eventually led her to writing and running a blog with one of her close friends. For more information, please visit her website and sign up for her newsletter.

Acknowledgments

As always, my loving husband and wonderful kids are the only reason I've been brave enough to write this story. Their support and encouragement means more to me than anything.

Next, I have to give a shout out to my girl, Kelley. You're more than my PA. You've become my best friend. You keep me organized and are always there to listen to me or bounce ideas off of. You're amazing, and I'd be lost without you.

All my stalkers, I appreciate your support and encouragement. You guys are my base, and I'm forever thankful for each and every one of you.

Kendra, we just met, but you are an awesome addition to my team. You are a rockstar, and I appreciate all your feedback and how you're willing to help in any way possible.

To all my readers and supporters, thank you for taking a chance on me.

Also by Jen L. Grey

THE PEARSON PROPHECY

Dawning Ascent

Enlightened Ascent

Reigning Ascent

Printed in Great Britain
by Amazon